DAT

Y0-CRG-065

SERENADE
Ilsa Mayr

From the moment Rachel Carradine hears the dark, rich tones of Blackie Madigan's alto saxophone, she knows her heart and her hard-fought, well-ordered life are in danger. As the daughter of a jazz musician, she knows the seductive power of the music just as she is familiar with the insecure, irregular, bohemian existence of the musicians. She escaped that lifestyle once and promised herself that nothing on earth could induce her to embrace it ever again. Yet hearing Blackie's Orpheus-like melodies, she is faced with the greatest temptation of her life.

But Blackie makes some dangerous assumptions about Rachel that threaten to derail their relationship before it even gets going. Unbeknownst to Rachel, Blackie is Blackstone J. Madigan, the entrepreneur behind the powerful conglomerate that owns Exotica, the company threatening Rachel's professional livelihood.

Mistaken identities, secrets, deception—hardly a harmonious beginning. Rachel and Blackie must see if their relationship can overcome these major obstacles and decide how much they're willing to risk and if it will be enough.

SERENADE

•

Ilsa Mayr

AVALON BOOKS

NEW YORK

Published by Thomas Bouregy & Co., Inc.
160 Madison Avenue, New York, NY 10016

Library of Congress Cataloging-in-Publication Data

Mayr, Ilsa.
    Serenade / Ilsa Mayr.
    p. cm.
    ISBN 978-0-8034-9865-5 (acid-free paper)
    1. Saxophonists—Fiction.   I. Title.

    PS3613.A97S47 2007
    813'.6—dc22

                                    2007026008

PRINTED IN THE UNITED STATES OF AMERICA
ON ACID-FREE PAPER
BY HADDON CRAFTSMEN, BLOOMSBURG, PENNSYLVANIA

To my aunts, Minna and Elisabeth, both faithful readers.

Chapter One

The note hung high, pure, perfect.

For a fraction of a second the smoke-filled, dim jazz club was hushed with awe. Then hands clapped enthusiastically, feet stomped vigorously, and whistles and calls exploded the reverent silence.

The saxophone player acknowledged the tribute with a slight inclination of his head and a smile. Even though Blackie Madigan had been receiving accolades for his performances for almost twelve months now, he was still as thrilled as he'd been the first time. He stepped out of the spotlight, allowing the pianist to ease into the next number.

Blackie took a long, thirsty pull from his tall, frosted glass and then surveyed the audience. In the upcoming number the saxophone echoed the piano only minimally, so he had a chance to look around. His blue eyes assessed the packed room and came to a saucer-eyed halt on the figure of a woman angling her way through the crowd toward the reserved table in front of the stage.

Her dark hair fell in loose, shining waves to her shoulders, sweeping the white fur stole thrown casually, carelessly over her left shoulder. The soft, luxurious fur matched the white gown of some rich, matte material, which clung to the feminine curves of her body.

For a moment he thought he'd been transported to the soundstage of a forties Hollywood movie set, and the jazz club had miraculously turned into a gin mill in Casablanca or Macao or Singapore. Espionage. Danger. A beautiful, mysterious woman whose arrival precipitated passion, jealousy, and love. Hedy Lamarr or perhaps Joan Bennett. Or Ava Gardner. No, Ava belonged to the fifties. It didn't matter. This woman was every bit as gorgeous as those legendary beauties.

The arpeggio flourish pulled him back to the present, and hastily he raised the sax to his lips to answer the piano in a brief glissando. What the hell was a woman like that doing in a jazz club dedicated, heart and soul, to serious music? The Blues in the Night was not some Chicago tourist trap that offered watered-down, bastardized jazz to please the ignorant and uninitiated.

Slumming, that's what she was doing. Some bored, rich socialite in search of a little excitement. Perhaps even a casual pickup. Though jazzmen didn't attract nearly the number of groupies that hung around rock musicians, they had their share. Not even his full mustache and close-cropped beard could hide the derisive slant of Blackie's mouth. He had no use for women like her. Yet, despite his disapproval, he continued to observe her.

Maybe he'd been wrong about her, he decided after a while. She listened intently, appreciatively, her gaze never leaving Evan Gregory at the piano. Evan was always worth watching, but in this particular number he was unquestionably spectacular. By grafting deep, dramatic bass notes onto ripe, full-blown right-hand chords, he projected vibes to the farthest reaches of the club and beyond.

Judging by her reaction, the dark-haired beauty did more than just respond emotionally to the music. She knew something about jazz and about the piano. Blackie's interest was piqued. He'd given up hope of meeting a woman who possessed both good looks and knowledge of jazz. Perhaps he'd been too hasty. Perhaps she was that rare combination he'd fantasized about for years. Perhaps . . . right, and the moon was made of green cheese, he mocked himself.

Still, he risked nothing but a rejection or disenchantment if he spoke to her. The disenchantment he was used to. Not the rejection. But that wasn't due to his irresistible charm; rather, he hadn't bothered to pursue any woman seriously for quite a while. He'd contented himself with women who were nice enough but didn't expect to be courted. They'd done all the pursuing.

Lithely he jumped off the low platform and crossed to her table. "Welcome to The Blues in the Night," he said. "Are you enjoying the music?"

Her startled gaze flew up to his face.

Looking into her eyes was like listening to a Charlie Parker solo—both could put a blister on a man's heart and a lien on his soul.

"Yes, I am. Very much," she said.

Good voice, Blackie noted, pleased. Middle register, clear, melodic. "Have you been here before?"

"No."

She hadn't invited him to sit down. "May I?" he asked, indicating a chair and straddling it before she could reply. No point in giving her a chance to refuse. "My name's Blackie Madigan. What's yours?" For a horrible moment he thought she would refuse to tell him her name.

"I'm Rachel Carradine."

Rachel. He digested that for a beat. The dark hair fit his image of what a Rachel should look like but not the eyes. In the dim light of the club he couldn't decide what color they were. They weren't blue or green. A fascinating combination of both? He'd have to see them in brighter light. How he was going to manage that, he didn't know yet. The lady definitely wasn't groupie material.

"You married?" he asked.

The blunt question seemed to surprise her. He wasn't sure how Rachel would react. Would she take into account that he was a musician, and musicians formed a category all their own? At least they liked to think so. Some people cut them some slack, and some didn't. He all but held his breath, waiting for her answer.

"I'm not married. Are you?"

"No." He grinned at her. He watched her observe

Evan, who was accepting a glass from a waitress. An anxious expression flitted across Rachel's face. "You okay?" he asked, looking at her carefully.

She flicked him a brief smile. "I'm fine."

Lovely smile, Blackie thought, and he continued to stare at her mouth. He'd been so taken with the contrast of her light eyes and dark hair that he hadn't noticed her mouth. *You're slipping, Madigan.* How could he not have noticed that tempting mouth?

It was at war with the rest of her face. It undid the classic look created by the symmetry of her bone structure and the cool, self-possessed air of her bearing. It proclaimed that its owner was quite capable of sensuous, sybaritic pleasures. Interesting, he thought, that though she'd applied makeup to the rest of her face, she'd left those luscious lips innocent of paint.

A waitress placed a drink in front of Blackie.

"Thanks." When he picked up the glass, he noticed Rachel's expression, which seemed disapproving.

"I'm old enough, you know," he said, pointing to his glass. "Besides, it's only ginger ale. I don't drink while I perform."

She looked away, apparently embarrassed at being caught, and took a sip of her cappuccino.

"How old are you?" he asked. When he saw her expression, he added hastily, "Don't get your dander up. It's just that I believe in getting down to basics. No sense in wasting time wondering and guessing."

"I don't like to waste time either. I'm thirty-four."

Blackie whistled softly. "You look younger."

Rachel inclined her head, acknowledging the compliment. "How old are you?"

She would match him question for question. Blackie liked that. It made the male-female game infinitely more interesting. "I'm thirty-six. Are you new to Chicago?"

"I've lived here for five months."

"And where did you live before?"

"New Jersey."

"Do you like it here?" he asked.

"Yes."

"I'm glad."

"Why?"

"It means you'll be staying for a while."

The waitress brought the cup of cappuccino Blackie had signaled for her to bring. He dug into a tight front pocket of his jeans but came up empty. He grinned at the waitress, who smiled back. "Put it on my tab, Nancy."

"Sure thing, Blackie."

He noted that the musicians were regrouping. "Looks like it's time for me to go back to work."

"Thanks for the coffee," Rachel said.

"You're welcome. First timers at The Blues in the Night can request a number," he said, guessing and hoping that she wouldn't know he'd just made that up.

"You being an alto horn player, can you play something by Charlie Parker?"

Blackie quirked an eyebrow at her. "Can I play something by Charlie Parker? Did the sun rise this morning? You ain't heard nothin' yet, darlin', till you hear me play," he said. Then he winked at her and leaped up onto the platform.

Rachel watched him walk away with a trace of regret until she realized what she was feeling. No matter how attractive Blackie Madigan was, he was also a musician, and hadn't she sworn she'd rather get multiple root canals than become involved with a musician again?

And wasn't it typical that he hadn't had any money? They never did. What they did have were tabs all over town. That she knew firsthand, having paid her father's tabs for years. And his remark that she was staying "for a while" was typical as well. Everything with him would be "for a while"—except the music.

Oh, but wasn't he something to watch? Cocksure, brash, and undeniably attractive. His teeth gleamed white against his dark beard and mustache. She had also noted the deep blue of his eyes, which were ringed by incredibly long, thick lashes. What rescued him from being too good-looking were his hawklike nose and strong chin.

He looked at ease, sure of himself and his appeal. Why shouldn't he? She knew from bitter experience that women threw themselves at musicians. Hadn't she been raised by one and briefly married to another? Even at sixty her father had no problems finding female companionship. Rachel glanced at him sitting at the piano, watched him take a coffee cup from the waitress and drink from it.

The familiar wave of anxiety surged through Rachel.

Let it be coffee. Just coffee, she prayed silently, fervently. Five months ago she had retrieved her father from yet another clinic, where the doctors had done their best to dry him out.

He had been on the wagon these five months she had spent relocating the offices of Athena, Inc., to Chicago from New Jersey, while keeping production, sales, and promotions of the cosmetics going. She'd had to find a place to live and adjust to the increased areas of responsibility Laura Croft, her boss, had delegated to her since marrying a diplomat attached to the British consulate and assuming many social obligations.

Rachel had also used those five months to get over her humiliating experience with Larry. Larry the louse, who'd dated her and wooed her only to get into the offices of Athena and steal the new face cream she was working on. He'd almost succeeded, the rat. By all that was holy, Laura should have accepted Rachel's resignation, but she hadn't. Instead she'd given her a promotion and a big raise.

Rachel had sworn that no man was ever going to get cosmetics secrets through her again. Not ever. She'd make sure she knew exactly what each prospective suitor did for a living, or she wouldn't date at all.

The sextet played for forty-five minutes without a break. Evan set the tone, but each man was master of his own instrument. In recent years her father had turned away from the cool jazz that so often drifted into precocity and had forged a style rooted in the bebop jazz of an earlier era. Rachel loved the hot and bluesy music. It was often plaintive and mournful but at the same time life-affirming.

Rachel watched Blackie Madigan launch into his solo. He could play. Lord, the man could play. He stood, feet clad in disreputable-looking sneakers and planted wide and firm, not needing to tap his foot, hearing the rhythm in his head and heart and soul. Whatever notes he saw, he saw behind his closed eyelids. Although he was unmistakably a Parker disciple, he had a style of his own. His alto sax, full-toned with a rich, slightly dark flavor, occasionally descended into wailing melancholy. His music leaped along Rachel's spine like tiny red-hot flames.

When the set ended, Blackie came to her and held out a hand. "Let's get some fresh air. It's awfully smoky in here." It was not a question, and it was not a command. It was a statement, a statement he expected her to comply with, and, uncharacteristically, she did. She, who was second in command at one of the finest and largest international cosmetics companies, followed this man into the dark night without a single question or a single qualm.

Shivering in the early-May night, Rachel pulled the stole closer around her shoulders.

"Cold?" Blackie asked. "Do you want my jacket?"

Rachel looked at the beige suede jacket he'd taken from a hook by the back door and shook her head. "No thanks. I'm fine."

With one finger Blackie touched her stole. "What kind of fur is this?"

"I don't know what it's called. It's synthetic."

"Synthetic?"

Rachel heard the surprise in his voice. She moved closer to the single lightbulb over the club's back entrance. "Look at it," she suggested, fingering the fur. "I would never condemn dozens of innocent, furry little creatures to death just so that I could flaunt some stupid, dubious status symbol. What kind of person do you think I am?"

Hearing the impassioned words and seeing the genuine indignation on her face left Blackie momentarily speechless. True, he himself had supported various efforts to save endangered species and to stop the slaughter of baby seals, but he'd never met a woman with Rachel's astonishing attitude toward owning a genuine fur coat.

Taking her up on her invitation, Blackie moved a step closer and touched the stole again. His sensitive musician's hands moved over the fur toward her slender neck. He was close enough to smell her scent, and he inhaled deeply.

"I love your perfume. It's mysterious, intoxicating, heady, and it gives me the same high I get when I hit perfect notes. What's it called?"

"It doesn't have a name yet."

"How come?"

Rachel debated briefly how much she should tell him. "I work for a cosmetics company, and they let us try out the new products before they're put on the market." That wasn't exactly a lie, she rationalized. Laura had asked her to wear her latest experimental creation.

"Looking the way you do, I bet you're the company's best PR for the cosmetics."

Since advertising was one of the departments she was in charge of, she could agree with him. "Mmm. I do some PR."

"I was surprised to see you come to the club alone. No steady man in your life?"

"No. How about you?"

"No steady woman."

"But you leave with a different woman every night, right?"

A scowl settled on his handsome face. His azure eyes turned cold. "Didn't you listen to my music? Do you think I'm that superficial?"

"No. I'm sorry. I didn't mean to hurt your feelings. I heard the intensity and the passion in your music," she admitted.

Blackie's hands, which still rested on the stole, moved to her throat. His thumbs stroked the silken skin. "What else did you hear?" he asked, his voice low.

A masculine siren call, which beckoned and lured. A seductive pull that roused a primitive, earthy response in her that would scandalize her if she could think straight. Which she couldn't. Not with him so close. Not with his fingers lingering on the spots where her pulse beat faster than the sextet's drums had. Not with his music still in her ears and her brain and her blood.

"What?" he repeated softly but insistently.

"You don't need me to tell you how good you are," she evaded.

"No, but your thinking I'm good isn't the same as your liking my playing."

For some reason it seemed important to him that she liked his music, and since she did, she saw no harm in admitting it. "Yes, I like the way you play. Isn't it obvious?"

"How do you mean, obvious?"

"I've never followed a man I just met into a parking lot. The only way I can explain that is that your music cast a spell over me. You're a modern version of the Pied Piper."

Blackie's blue eyes looked steadily into hers. When she attempted to lower her head, his thumbs moved under her chin and held her upturned face steady. "You're not half bad at casting a spell yourself," he claimed.

She'd been called many things in her life but never bewitching. "Me?"

"Yes, you."

Everything was moving way too fast. The cool spring air had cleared her head of the music and the smoke. She stepped away from Blackie just as the door behind her opened a crack.

"Hey, Blackie. It's time to start another set."

Rachel recognized the man as the drummer.

"Okay, Poco. I'll be right there," Blackie answered. "You're staying, right?" he said to her. "Please," he added, his eyes pleading.

"Yes." She was staying because she hadn't had a chance to talk to her father yet. Otherwise she'd not only leave, she'd positively sprint as fast and as far as she could.

Back at her table, Rachel couldn't believe what she'd done, how she'd behaved. She'd followed a man she didn't know into the dark night. And she had almost let him kiss her. She had little doubt that if Poco hadn't interrupted them, Blackie Madigan would have kissed her. To make matters worse, if that was possible, Blackie was a musician. Worse still, he was the player of an instrument that made her toes curl and her scalp tingle. To Rachel there was nothing more seductive than the sound of the alto sax. Knowing all that, how could she have allowed herself to follow him?

She should have told him she wasn't interested the moment he'd come to her table. She'd had enough practice turning a man down that she could do it without hurting his feelings. But no. Instead she'd abandoned herself to emotion, and that invariably led to disaster.

What could she do? Analyze the problem, propose solutions, and implement what appeared to be the best one. That's what she always did on her job, and it worked. The problem was that she was attracted to Blackie Madigan, a man totally unsuitable, a man so dangerous and threatening to her well-being, her peace of mind, that all sorts of warning bells clanged in her head. Yet despite those warning signals a tiny, traitorous voice in her heart asked if Blackie really was bad for her.

Rachel's thoughts turned back to that other saxo-
phonist she'd been attracted to all those years ago.
She'd fallen in love with Earl Carradine. She'd loved
him with all the purity and innocence of first love. She'd
married him in her youthful innocence and ignorance,
believing that he'd loved her too. Perhaps he had loved
her, at least as much as he was capable of loving anyone.

The music had come first, though. It always did. She
could have lived with that, she thought, but she couldn't
live with the casual infidelities and the drinking, just as
her mother hadn't been able to live with them. Unlike
her mother, Rachel had been smart enough to end the
torment. Her marriage had lasted less than a year.

Remembering the past had a deeply sobering effect
on her. Rachel took a shuddering breath and knew what
she had to do.

As long as her father played at The Blues in the
Night, she had to come periodically to see him. Actually, it was more like checking up on him, even if she
didn't like to think of it that way. She knew that he
liked her to come to hear him play, knew that her presence had a beneficial influence on him. Evan loved her.
She knew that, just as she knew that the only thing she
couldn't do was stop him from going on a bender, she
reflected sadly.

The music claimed her attention. Her father launched
into an Erroll Garner piece that was one of her favorites.
There was probably no other pianist who could dupli-
cate that unique Garner right-hand rubato the way Evan
did. As always when she listened to her father, she felt

both proud and happy. When Blackie's sax answered the piano's challenge with supreme confidence and beauty, Rachel steeled her heart against its Orpheus-like, magic, seductive power. That's how it had to be. She forced herself not to look at Blackie.

As soon as the set ended, Rachel rushed to her father's side and sat down beside him on the piano bench.

"That was great, Evan." She threw her arms around her father and kissed his cheek. An only child, she'd called her father what the adults around him called him. He'd liked that, so she continued to use his first name.

"I played that number for you, sugar."

"Thanks. I'm sorry I couldn't get here on opening night, but I had to fly to Jersey and spend several days at the old plant," she explained.

"You told me, and it's okay."

"I came as soon as I could leave the business dinner I had to attend tonight."

"You look nice. A little dressed up for the place, but nice."

"I know," Rachel said, glancing at the informally dressed audience, "but I didn't want to miss any more of the music than I had to."

The waitress brought a drink and offered it to Evan. "Would you like something?" he asked Rachel.

"No, thanks, but I'll take a sip of yours," she said.

"Sure." Evan handed her the glass.

Rachel drank cautiously. *Club soda, thank heaven,* she thought, relieved, and she took another sip. She gave the glass back to Evan.

"What do you think of the combo?" he asked.

"I think you guys are great together, don't you?"

"Yes. I believe this is one of the best groups I've ever played with. I really lucked out when I learned about them at the recovery center."

That was good news. Whenever Evan played with a group of musicians who were all recovering from some addiction or other and supported one another's efforts to remain clean, the chances of his staying sober increased dramatically. "What do you know about them?" she asked, her voice studiedly casual.

"You mean what do I know about Blackie Madigan, don't you?" There was an amused twinkle in Evan's shrewd eyes.

"You think you know me so well, don't you," Rachel said, poking her elbow playfully into his ribs.

"Don't I, sugar? I was there when you were born, missy," he reminded her. "About Blackie . . ." Evan paused thoughtfully. "Funny, I know quite a bit about the other guys' personal lives but not about Blackie's. All I know about him is that he's from Baltimore, and I think someone said he wasn't married."

"I know that. He told me."

"Oh? You got that personal already?" Evan's bushy eyebrows rose.

"The man believes in getting down to the nitty-gritty," Rachel said, her tone dry.

"That's not a bad way to be. I think he's a good man. He's dependable, which is a quality not often found in musicians, as you know from experience." Evan's voice was wry, and he flashed her a small, self-deprecating, apologetic smile.

Rachel linked her arm through her father's in a comforting gesture. "Are you through for the night?"

"Officially, yes, but Jawbone's coming, and we'll jam for a while. Want to stay? He'd be glad to see you."

Rachel glanced at her slim gold watch. "No, I'd better not. Say hello to him for me. How is he?"

"On the wagon, just like me."

Jawbone was Evan's oldest friend and one of the best jazz trumpeters around when he was sober. Rachel rose from the bench, and so did Evan.

"I'll be back soon, Evan," she promised. They hugged each other affectionately.

"Good night, sugar."

Rachel turned and met Blackie's gaze. She recoiled from the cold fury she saw in his burning eyes. She inclined her head in a mute gesture of good-bye. Not understanding his anger but puzzled and alarmed by it, she hurried out of the club.

Chapter Two

Rachel leaned back in her chair and stared idly out of her office window. Why had Blackie Madigan been so angry with her last night? She'd mulled and stewed about that plenty but could come up with no answer. One moment he'd gazed at her with enough heat to melt her teeth, and the next he acted as if he'd like nothing better than to shake her till her bones rattled.

True, she had avoided looking at him during the last set they played, but surely that wasn't enough to make him so furious. It might have dented his ego a little, but he was self-assured enough that that wouldn't have been sufficient to provoke such a strong reaction.

In a gesture of disgust, she threw down the pencil she'd been toying with. Why did his anger bother her? Why should she care what he thought? Hadn't she decided to have nothing to do with the man?

Resolutely she slipped into her navy, shawl-collared

suit jacket, picked up her papers and her purse, and headed for the conference room and the weekly staff meeting. Even though Laura was absent, Rachel did not take the chair at the head of the table. She sat in her usual place and called the meeting to order. One by one the department heads gave their reports. Laura had allowed each of them five minutes, and Rachel stuck with the practice. It kept them from wasting time.

"Thank you," she said when the last report was given. "Everything looks good, but we have a major problem." Rachel could feel the tension rise in the room. "Our archrival, Exotica Cosmetics, has done it again."

Henry, Athena's financial genius and professional worrier, popped the teeth-marked stem of his pipe into his mouth and clamped down on it hard enough to add another set of impressions before he even heard the rest of what Rachel had to say.

"Exotica is coming out with a cheap imitation of Amour, which they had the gall to call Amore."

Everybody in the room spoke at once.

"They can't do that. . . ."

"Let's sue them. . . ."

"Does Laura know . . ."

"Please." Rachel held up a hand, and the angry voices quieted. "I'm as upset as you are, and so is Laura. I've consulted with Sam Thornton, but we have no grounds for a lawsuit."

"No grounds?" sputtered Henry indignantly.

"No. Exotica doesn't come right out and say that

their perfume is as *good* as ours. Only that it costs less than the expensive brand."

"Isn't it enough? This will ruin us," Henry prophesied.

His hangdog expression looked even more dour than usual, Rachel noticed. "No, it won't, and let's not assume a defeatist attitude." From her purse Rachel took a bottle of the rival scent and set it on the table. "A disgruntled ex-employee of Exotica gave me an experimental sample," she explained.

"My God. They even had the nerve to use the same kind of lettering for the name," Jay Meyer, head of advertising, muttered, stunned.

"Why don't we pass it around and let the women sample it?" Rachel suggested.

Peggy, her executive assistant, dabbed a little on her wrist and passed the bottle.

"It sure smells a lot like Amour," Jay said.

"We're going to fight back." The bottle had made the rounds. "Thirty minutes before I came to this meeting, I dabbed a little Amour on one wrist and some of Amore on the other. I want each of you to write down on which wrist I have what."

Slowly Rachel made her way around the table, fairly certain what the outcome of her impromptu test would be. "Okay. Pass the pieces of paper to Peggy, who'll tally the results."

It took only a few moments. "The votes are unanimous. You're wearing Amour on your right wrist and the imitation on your left," Peggy announced.

"That's correct. None of you had any trouble telling the difference between them. Why?"

"Because our perfume smells better," Henry said promptly and proudly.

"It doesn't change, the way this stuff does once you put it on," Peggy said, wrinkling her nose at the imitation scent she'd put on her wrist.

"Amour lasts much longer. The stuff on your left wrist is beginning to fade after only half an hour," Jay explained.

One by one they gave their reasons, and they were all excellent.

"Laura and I agree that we need a new ad campaign that will state all the things you've been telling me. Jay, drop everything else and get started. Exotica is close to marketing their imitation, so we won't beat them to the punch, but I want us to refute their claims before they've had a chance to sink into the public consciousness."

"Right," Jay said, his mind already clicking off possibilities.

"I hate those sons of bitches at Exotica," Henry grumbled.

"None of us loves them, exactly, but look at it this way: their shenanigans keep us on our toes," Rachel consoled.

"I still maintain that Exotica ripped off the formula of our Springtime astringent and hired Larry Stanton, even though he never confessed who'd employed him," Henry said broodingly.

"Probably. But we never could prove anything against them," Rachel pointed out.

"Vigilante justice looks better and better to me all the time," Henry mumbled, and he walked off, holding his pipe like a lethal weapon.

Rachel and Peggy exchanged expressive looks and followed him out of the conference room. Henry was so predictable.

"Be still," Rachel ordered, one hand holding the wet dog while she reached for the shampoo with the other. "I told you when you moved in with me that a weekly bath was part of the deal."

The small black-and-brown dog looked at her with pleading, long-suffering, gold-colored eyes. She worked the shampoo through Piccolo's short coat and rinsed him with several pitchers of warm water.

"All done," she crooned cheerfully, and she toweled him thoroughly, though she knew the moment she released him, he would shake himself vigorously.

He did. Then he shot out of the room like a rocket.

Rachel chuckled and cleaned up the laundry room, where this weekly ordeal took place. She noted that she was every bit as wet as the freshly bathed dog. She showered and changed into a long, flowing robe.

As soon as she sat down on the sofa in the living room, Callie hopped into her lap, beating the other cat to this coveted spot by a second. Cleo sent her sister a withering look and curled up on the sofa beside Rachel, who was kept busy stroking the silky felines. Ordinarily this was a relaxing time, the rhythmic purring of the cats acting as a natural tranquilizer. Not tonight. Rachel was as restless as the moaning wind that knocked the branches of the lilac tree against the window.

The impending storm was a good reason she shouldn't go to The Blues in the Night, she told herself. Another good reason was that she didn't want to face Blackie Madigan.

That wasn't true. She was dying to see him again, even though she knew she shouldn't. Actually, she was going to see her father. She'd stayed away from the club for three nights, and if she didn't drop by soon, Evan would worry. Thinking along those lines, she convinced herself to go.

Rachel picked up Callie and set her on the sofa, ignoring the reproachful look in the topaz eyes. Upstairs she changed outfits three times before she settled on narrow black slacks and a belted, ruby red tunic.

When she parked behind the club, the first fat raindrops splattered against the concrete, forcing her to make a mad dash for the door. The smooth, sensuous tones of Blackie's saxophone washed over her as soon as she entered the club, and a ripple of pure pleasure surged through her veins. She recognized the tune. "The Intimacy of the Blues"—a particular favorite of hers.

She stopped just inside the door and listened. She'd fight her way to the front during the combo's break. In one of the numbers Blackie and Jumbo, the trumpet player, dueled back and forth in a lively, humorous manner.

Blackie knew almost to the second when Rachel Carradine entered the club. He'd been waiting for her to return, waiting with his anger, his temper, and his desire to see her barely leashed. He watched her hurry toward Evan, watched her hug him, smile at him, sit down next to him on the piano bench, and take a sip of his drink. That intimate gesture inflamed him. Damn her.

How could she have flirted with him that way when she was obviously another man's woman? He'd have to have a talk with Rachel of the loose morals, he promised himself almost gleefully. Blackie had plans, big plans, for the combo, and he needed Evan Gregory. He wouldn't let some sweet-talking, conniving female upset the gifted pianist and drive him back to the bottle.

"Oh, Evan, I think that's wonderful!" Rachel cried out happily, and she hugged her father. "A recording date? I've dreamed of and prayed for that."

"Me too, sugar. Madigan's the one who's arranging it," Evan said, grinning broadly.

"Did I hear my name mentioned?" Blackie asked, joining the happy couple at the piano. The way Rachel smiled at him warmed his heart, but then he saw her arm linked through Evan's, and the warmth chilled into ice.

"Yes. Evan told me that you've found a producer and arranged a studio date. I think that's fantastic."

Her light eyes shone with joy and happiness as she looked at him, and for the first time in his life Blackie knew what it meant to covet another man's woman. Didn't Evan notice how warmly Rachel was smiling at him, Blackie? Was love really blind?

Damnation. This complicated everything just at a time when they all needed to concentrate on nothing but the music. He'd have to speak to that sweet witch and set her straight about a few things.

"How soon will you get into the studio?" Rachel asked.

"In a week."

"It'll give us just enough time to rehearse," Evan said, and he flexed his fingers.

"You already sound awfully good," Rachel said, her eyes shining with loyalty.

"That's because you're a little prejudiced." Evan patted her arm.

"Maybe just a tad," Rachel replied with a happy smile.

Blackie watched this affectionate exchange with an expression that matched his name.

Evan waved to someone and stood up. "Excuse me. I'll just go over there to say hello."

Rachel and Blackie watched his still-slim figure as he approached the table of two eagerly smiling women.

Blackie sat down next to Rachel, his thigh pressing against hers. She didn't move. She couldn't. The piano bench, which had been wide enough when she shared it with Evan, now seemed narrow.

"You don't mind?" Blackie asked, inclining his head in the direction of the table from which merry laughter rang.

Rachel looked at the two women, who were near

Evan's age, well dressed, and prosperous-looking. They didn't look like the type who'd exploit him. "No, I don't mind. Why should I?"

This close her eyes looked gray, Blackie thought, fascinated by them. Their expression was guileless. She really didn't mind that Evan was flirting with the two women who came regularly to hear him play. What in the hell kind of a relationship did Rachel and Evan have anyway? Was she that sure of him? Or did she care that little?

He looked at the two women closely. True, they were a good deal older than Rachel, but they were still quite attractive. If Rachel were his, and she sat with two men—even if they were a lot older—and enjoyed their company as much as Evan was enjoying the ladies', he'd be over there in a flash, rearranging some faces. If the tables were turned, he hoped Rachel would be a little annoyed with him too.

"Don't worry about Evan," Rachel said. "He can take care of himself." She smiled at Blackie and laid a reassuring hand on his arm.

At the touch, warmth zigzagged up his arm straight to his heart.

Rachel wished she could reach up and touch his beard. She sensed that it would feel silky against her face if he kissed her, and she longed to feel its texture. He wasn't so undisguisedly furious with her tonight, but she felt anger, as well as other powerful emotions, sizzling beneath the surface. She met his hot gaze, and the air fairly crackled with tension between them. She flicked her tongue over her suddenly dry lips.

Blackie wished she hadn't done that. His eyes focused on her mouth. It drove him crazy to look at those full lips and not kiss them. As if she sensed the danger, Rachel spoke.

"So, tell me about the studio," she requested.

With difficulty Blackie forced himself to speak. "There's not much to tell. It'll need some modification to suit our needs, but nothing I can't handle."

He sounded so sure of himself. He had the take-charge attitude she met in business all the time but had never encountered among musicians. She wondered what he'd done before he exploded on the Chicago jazz scene a year ago, as Evan described it. He'd obviously played before. No one acquired such expertise on an instrument overnight. Where and why had he hidden his incredible talent? The man was full of secrets. An alarm resonated in Rachel's brain.

Evan rejoined them, looking cheerful and pleased with himself.

"I have to go," Rachel announced, glancing at her watch. "I want to stop at the clinic to see how Trio is getting along."

"Is that what you named him?" Evan asked, amused.

Rachel turned to Blackie to explain. "Several weeks ago I visited friends in the country, and we found this poor cat with his left hind paw in one of those awful traps. Oooh, if I ever meet someone who sets those traps, I'll be arrested for aggravated assault, and he'll be in the hospital for months," she ground out.

"To stop a lecture on the evils of trapping, let me

continue," Evan offered. "The vet had to amputate the cat's leg." He turned to his daughter and looked at her suspiciously. "You're going to keep him, aren't you?"

"What else can I do? Who's going to adopt a three-legged cat?" she asked, defending her action.

"Shoot, one more creature to share your house with," Evan complained. "How many was it the last time I stayed the night?"

That did it. Blackie barely leashed the violence that swept through him. He positively seethed with jealousy and resentment.

"You exaggerate," Rachel said, and she kissed her father's cheek. She smiled, wished them a good night, and left.

Blackie watched her gently swaying hips and made a fast decision. *No sense putting it off,* he thought, and he hurried after her. He caught up with her just outside the door.

"Not so fast," he ordered, clamping a hand onto her shoulder.

Rachel gasped, turned, and looked at him accusingly. "You scared me half to death."

That wasn't all he wanted to do to her. "Let's set a few ground rules."

"About what?"

"About you and Evan."

"Oh?"

Blackie looked into her arresting eyes and could no longer distinguish the warring emotions that tore his insides into bloody shreds. He took a deep breath to steady himself.

"The recording session is extremely important, and I won't allow anything to interfere with it," he warned.

"I have no intention of interfering," Rachel said, puzzled.

"Just don't. Evan is the best jazz pianist alive when he's not drinking, which hasn't been all that often in recent years."

As if she didn't know, Rachel thought.

"I want to get him into the studio before he goes on another binge. His talent's unique—we've got to capture it for posterity."

"I agree totally."

"So don't play any of the usual games that might drive him to drink."

"What?" Rachel had no idea what Madigan was talking about. There wasn't another human being on this earth who'd tried harder than she had to keep her father from drinking.

"Don't play the innocent with me. There'll be no fooling around with other men, including me. There'll be no spending sprees to bankrupt Evan. There'll be nothing from you, sugar," he said, stressing the "sugar" sarcastically, "to upset him in the least. If there is, I'll come after you, and you won't like what I'll have to do. Is that understood?"

Taking her stunned silence for agreement, he said, "Good." He flashed a last dark look at her and stalked back into the club.

Rachel stared at the back door for several minutes after it closed on the tall, furious figure. What on earth was Blackie Madigan talking about? Spending sprees that would bankrupt Evan? Fooling around? Rachel doing *anything* to push him off the wagon? The man didn't make any sense. *He's been blowing that horn so hard that not enough oxygen has gotten to his brain,* she thought facetiously. She shook her head and drove off to the clinic, thoroughly bewildered.

Inside the club Blackie paused, hands clenched into fists, trying to get his temper and his emotions under control, which wasn't easy. He'd made a royal mess of things, he berated himself. He shouldn't have sought out Rachel in the first place. That's the last thing on God's good earth he should have done. She belonged to a man he admired and liked more than any other. He had no right to want her. He called himself seven different kinds of a fool. But that was water under the bridge.

The important thing was what he was going to do in the future. What in heaven's name could he do about Rachel? The easiest thing would be to seduce her and so prove to Evan that she was no good, but that might drive Gregory back to the bottle—the one thing Blackie didn't want to happen. He could try to buy her off, but that might reap the same result. Blast Evan Gregory and his penchant for women decades younger than himself.

Blackie ran a thumbnail over his mustache in a gesture of frustration. There was nothing he could do, he concluded, except watch that Rachel didn't take Evan to the cleaners. Not like that exotic dancer, Nana, who'd stripped the man barer than a buzzard picks a carcass. Evan had told him about Nana a few nights ago after a lengthy jam session.

Blackie scowled, remembering a similar incident in his own past. After his picture had appeared on the cover of *Financial News* as one of a new breed of entrepreneurs, he'd been flush with success and pride, feeling that the world was his oyster. At only twenty-five, he hadn't had much experience with sly, manipulative women.

What easy prey he'd been for Delores, he thought wryly. A chicken begging to be plucked. A lamb dying to be shorn. When she was through with him, she'd left for Hollywood with a new nose, straight teeth, a bigger bust, and an expensive wardrobe. She'd taught him a lesson he'd never forgotten: women weren't to be trusted, especially if they knew who he really was. As Blackstone J. Madigan he was never sure if they liked him for himself or for his money. Probably some of each, with the money tilting the scales, he reflected cynically.

Rachel posed a problem. He'd have to watch her like a hawk. That also meant he'd have to watch her being with Evan, and that would tear his guts out. Why did he have to find her so compellingly, so consumingly attractive? During the past two days she'd invaded his mind like a powerful virus. He couldn't shake her. He muttered every vile word he knew, and he knew many, before he rejoined the sextet for their last set of the evening.

"Want to go out for a bite to eat?" Evan asked

Blackie when they were done. The musicians were packing up their instruments, ready to call it a night.

"Don't you want to rush home?" Blackie asked.

"Not particularly," Evan said, lowering the piano lid.

That was odd, Blackie thought. If Rachel were waiting for him, he'd sprint all the way home to make love to her. Of course, Evan was no spring chicken. The juices probably slowed down a bit as you got older.

Blackie glanced at his watch. "I can't, Evan. I have to meet my . . . brother." He'd almost blown it by saying "my attorney." His attorney was also his older brother, so he really wouldn't have lied, but he was trying to keep his business career separate from his music. He preferred the men in the combo to think of him as a fellow musician, not as an entrepreneur.

Since he hadn't driven tonight, Blackie headed out of the club and down the block to where the limousine was waiting for him.

The chauffeur opened the door for him. "Good evening, Mr. Madigan."

"Evening, Horace." Blackie slid into the backseat next to his brother and opposite his executive assistant.

"How did it go tonight?" Ben asked.

"The music was fine," Blackie said a little curtly.

When he didn't elaborate, his brother opened his briefcase and pulled out a folder. He handed it to Blackie. "As soon as you sign on the dotted lines, you'll be the proud owner of PRX Studio and a couple million poorer. Did you have to buy the studio? Isn't that carrying your hobby to an extreme?" Ben asked.

"No, and it's not just a hobby. It's an avocation, a calling."

Blackie knew his brother didn't understand his passion for jazz. He never had and never would. Just as his parents hadn't and still didn't. He'd begged to be allowed to study music, but his father had insisted that Blackie major in business administration. He remembered his father's indignant, "What? Study music and starve?"

Perhaps it had been for the best after all. The business major got him into computers and designing sophisticated software. It made him a millionaire at an early age and allowed him to indulge his love for music. Blackie studied the papers with his usual concentration and signed them.

"The studio's an investment. We're not the only group who will use it, but by owning it I can produce what I want without hassles from anyone," Blackie explained. He had to have artistic freedom, and he could afford to buy it. "I don't want anyone to know that I own the studio," he cautioned the two men.

They dropped Ben off at his fashionable Lake Shore Drive address, and Blackie turned his attention to his assistant Curtis Shafer. Blackie employed two assistants, one for the late-night hours and one for the afternoons. They discussed meetings to be scheduled, pending contracts, and new software programs. By the time Blackie arrived home, it was four in the morning.

Perhaps one of these days he'd sell most of his companies, invest the proceeds, and become a full-time musician. That appealed to him more and more. Perhaps he was getting too old to hold down two full-time jobs, he thought, and he ran a weary hand over his beard.

His current lifestyle also precluded any kind of meaningful relationship with a woman. He hadn't minded that until now, he realized. His lifestyle didn't really matter now either, since the woman he wanted couldn't be his, he thought. He tasted the bitterness in his mouth.

Why couldn't she? Rachel didn't seem to be deeply in love with Evan, and, come to think of it, Evan didn't act like a man crazy in love either.

Blackie was shocked at his treacherous thoughts and dismissed them guiltily. His friendship with Evan was much more important than a fling, no matter how passionate, with a woman. He spent a long time trying to convince himself of that.

Usually Blackie was so tired that he fell asleep as soon as his head hit the pillow, but not tonight. He couldn't get the picture of Rachel out of his head. How much he wanted her and how much he couldn't have her. Perhaps he couldn't have her now, but what about the future?

Perhaps they'd meet in another place, another time. Grimly he tried to hold on to a faint glimmer of hope as he stared into the darkness. When the sun rose, his eyes were red-rimmed and his heart heavy.

Chapter Three

They slumped around the conference table, which was covered with coffee cups, overflowing ashtrays, and papers. Jay wadded up his latest effort and shot it into the wastebasket. They had been brainstorming for most of the afternoon, trying to come up with a slogan lauding the superiority of Amour.

Rachel walked to a window and watched the rain-drops slide down the glass. She was in a blue funk, and she didn't really need a psychologist to tell her why. What she ought to do was march herself over to The Blues in the Night and demand an explanation. How dare Blackie Madigan assume that she would do anything to drive her father to drink? The nerve of the man!

Rachel tried to estimate how many bottles of liquor she'd ferreted from ingenious hiding places and emptied down the drain during the years she'd lived with her father. Or how often she'd pleaded with him, cajoled, argued, begged. How often she'd bailed him out, paid his fines and his bills. Or how often she'd let herself hope that the latest cure would last.

Madigan had no right to fault her behavior where Evan was concerned, and tonight she'd set him straight. Angry determination surged through her, stiffening her shoulders, her spine. It was a different Rachel who turned from the window and faced her staff, who were arguing, tempers running short.

"Okay," she said, and the voices quieted. "What is the one thing Athena is known for above all others?"

"Quality," Jay said.

"Purity," Peggy added.

"Exactly. For this campaign we'll concentrate on quality," Rachel stated. "I've talked with Laura, and she wants to go all out on this one. Magazine ads, giveaways, and a TV commercial. Let's start with the magazine ad. How about a short slogan like 'Quality Endures'?"

"Yeah. Under it a picture of a bottle of Amour on a piece of antique lace," Archie, their photographer, suggested.

"Or sitting on a fine silver tray," Jay said.

"Or on top of a leather-bound volume of Shakespeare's sonnets," Peggy volunteered.

"Those are all possibilities," Rachel agreed. "What other slogan could we come up with to convince people to go for the genuine, the original, rather than the imitation?"

"I know," Jay said, his face animated. "Let's juxtapose two objects, one clearly much more desirable than the other, and ask which they'd rather have. Then one word underneath it: 'Exactly!' And under that 'Amour'. Let me show you," he said, and he turned to the portable chalkboard. He sketched as he talked. "We could have a Faberge egg side by side with a plain chicken egg, with the caption under it, 'Which would you rather have?' Below that, 'Exactly. Just as you would rather have Amour'."

"Not bad," Rachel mused.

Suddenly everyone in the room came up with a suggestion.

"A rowboat and a yacht."

"A Bentley and a beat-up jalopy."

"A diamond necklace and plastic beads."

"A hunk and a scarecrow."

Rachel burst into laughter when she realized what Peggy had said, and so did everyone else. When she could, she said, "I think we'll skip that one, but I like the others. Jay, why don't you work along those lines and get some sketches ready. Peggy and I will see what we can come up with for the giveaway."

"Sorry about that," Peggy said as the women walked out together. "It slipped out." She grinned a little sheepishly.

Rachel grinned back. "Daydreaming about a hunk, huh?"

"All the time. Don't you?"

Lately she was. About one hunk in particular. One blue-eyed, black-haired, black-hearted hunk who sent out enough conflicting signals to render the nation's radar system inoperative. Rachel hated ambiguity. Her track record with men wasn't that terrific when everything was clear and aboveboard. For the clever, successful businesswoman she considered herself to be, she was a little dense about men.

With all the men she'd gone out with since her divorce, there just hadn't been that spark. It certainly was there with Blackie. Was it ever. She looked at him and felt warm and shivery at the same time, and when she listened to his music, she thought the stars were falling out of the sky. She'd better watch herself, or she'd be in over her head. She sighed.

"Problems with a hunk?" Peggy asked.

"Don't know yet. I'll let you know when I do."

Rachel didn't find out that night because she never made it to The Blues in the Night. An emergency at the New Jersey plant forced her to catch an evening plane. When she returned home three days later, there was an invitation on her answering machine from Evan. It was the combo's night off, and he was throwing a party.

A party. The word set her heart to beating anxiously. With everyone around him drinking, Evan could be led astray. She'd better attend it, even though she'd prefer a hot bath and a quiet evening at home with her pets.

They were always so glad to see her. Piccolo jumped up and down, barking like crazy, and the cats, after hissing at the dog to stop his loud antics, rubbed themselves against her legs. Although she knew that her part-time maid took good care of them, she felt a twinge of guilt at leaving them. It was almost as bad as being a working mother, Rachel thought.

She wondered if Blackie would be at the party. Probably, she decided, and her heart leaped joyously. Then she forced herself to be rational and practical. It would be better for her if the man wasn't there. Safer. For a moment she considered calling Sam Thornton, her attorney and friend, to escort her as he'd done many times in the past, but, glancing at her watch, she decided against it.

Being in the beauty business had conditioned Rachel to look flawless and meticulous at all times, but she found herself dressing with even greater care than usual. That discovery didn't please her. "Fool," she threw at her reflection in the mirror of her dressing table. She grabbed her evening clutch and left.

Blackie's heart skipped a beat when he heard her voice. So, she'd come. Part of him didn't want her there, didn't want to feel the pain and the jealousy that coursed through him. Rachel Carradine was just a woman, he told himself. An ordinary woman. Half of the world's population were women. Sure, and the *Mona Lisa* was just a painting, and Charlie "Bird" Parker just a horn player. Blackie raised his head to look at her. He watched Evan rush to greet her.

"Hi, sugar. I was hoping you'd come."

"Evan." They hugged. "Thanks for asking me."

"Why wouldn't I invite my best girl?"

"You look well," Rachel observed.

"I'm still stone-cold sober," he assured her.

"Who's the woman talking to Blackie?" Rachel asked.

"That's Donna. She's a pretty good blues singer. Or she would be, if she'd get serious about it. So far she's only toyed with the idea. Maybe we can persuade her to sing," Evan said.

Great, Rachel thought, and her mood took another nosedive. Not only was the woman attractive, she was musical as well.

Evan hit the opening chords of "Lover Man," and though Donna was no Billie Holiday, she was good. Jawbone's trumpet joined in, and Rachel knew they were off to a musical evening.

She moved back, allowing the musicians to crowd around the piano. For the first time in her life she wished she had some musical ability so that she could join in. She closed her eyes and listened, swaying to the sensuous blues melodies, savoring the plaintive lyrics. Love and longing . . . pain and passion . . . tears and torment.

"It always comes down to that, doesn't it?"

Rachel's eyes flew open. She hadn't heard Blackie Madigan approach. With one shoulder propped against a wall, his back was turned to the piano, shielding her from view.

"What comes down to what?" she managed to ask, wondering if she should put more distance between them.

"What the blues are about. Love and passion."

"Also tears and betrayal," Rachel said softly. "Don't forget that."

"Sounds like a warning."

"Just listen to the lyrics," she suggested with a slight shrug. "You didn't bring your saxophone?"

"No. I thought I'd give my lips a rest," he said. *At least from the horn.* There were some activities they'd be only too eager to engage in, he thought, looking at Rachel's lush mouth. Tonight she wore lip gloss that matched the vivid pink of her dress. Would she taste like strawberries?

Rachel felt his intense stare, and her pulse leaped crazily. Why wasn't he with the others around the piano? Finally she dared to look at him. Their gazes met and held.

Her eyes were a soft gray tonight, Blackie decided, their expression a little wary and a little expectant, and he knew he would kiss her.

Rachel's breath caught when he laid a well-shaped musician's hand against the wall beside her face. He leaned closer, and his face filled her vision. She meant to protest the unsuitability of time and place, but his lambent eyes rendered her mute.

It was a whisper of a kiss, sweet and gentle and full of promise, and it left her curiously shaken. Blackie moved his mouth a hair's breadth from hers before he kissed her again. Rachel's heartbeat rivaled Evan's staccato chords on the piano.

"Stop that, Blackie," she whispered. "We're with a roomful of people, for heaven's sake."

"So?"

"So, we're not a couple of teenagers who're at the mercy of their hormones." Rachel moved her head away from him, only to be stopped by his hand resting against the wall.

"Speak for your own hormones, sweetheart," he whispered, a wicked light dancing in his azure eyes. "Mine are practicing the scales all the way from a low *C* to a high *A*."

In spite of herself she had to smile.

Fascinated, he watched her sweet, full lips part, and he suppressed a groan. He'd donate a year's worth of profits from Obsidian International if he could kiss that tempting mouth to his heart's content. He shut his eyes against temptation, but it didn't help. Somebody had tattooed the outline of her mouth on the inside of his eyelids. In the warmth of the room, the perfume Rachel wore mingled with the scent of her skin and hair and assailed his senses powerfully.

"Let's get out of here," he suggested.

"It would be rude. I just arrived."

His eyes snapped open. He couldn't believe he'd suggested that. He was a guest in Evan's apartment, and he'd had the temerity to ask his host's woman to leave with him. With a friend like him, Evan didn't need any enemies. Talk about being a lowlife!

Then Rachel's words registered with a jolt. The only reason she wouldn't leave with him was because it would be rude. Not because it would be immoral or faithless or would hurt Evan, but because it would be a breach of good manners. What a pair they were. Perhaps they really deserved each other.

He was doing it again, Rachel noticed. Hot one

moment, cold the next. He had physically moved back from her as if she'd suddenly broken out with leprosy, and the look on his face . . . If it would make any sense under the circumstances, she'd describe it as loathing. But that made no sense whatsoever.

"What's wrong, Blackie?"

"You have to ask that?"

That *was* an expression of disgust on his face, she realized, puzzled. "Yes, I do. I don't see what's wrong."

"You don't see anything wrong?" he exploded. "Evan's less than fifteen feet away, in heaven's name, and you don't see anything wrong? I don't believe you," he snapped, backing away from her with a disbelieving shake of his head.

Practically openmouthed, Rachel watched him turn and storm over to the makeshift bar and pour a slug of whiskey into a glass. He tossed it down in one gulp. She flinched. The last thing Rachel wanted to do was drive a man to drink. Any man. What had she done wrong?

Going over what they had said and done didn't help. Unless Blackie thought that her father would disapprove of their going out together. Surely Blackie knew how highly Evan thought of him. Did he think she had to ask Evan's permission to date? He knew she was thirty-four years old, for crying out loud. Surely he couldn't hold such archaic ideas.

That did it. She was going to corner Evan and demand that he get her some information on Blackie Madigan. Maybe the man had severe emotional problems. Just because he was a brilliant musician didn't guarantee that he was normal. How else could the Jekyll-Hyde changes in his behavior be explained?

It was impossible to get Evan alone. When he wasn't playing the piano, he was being a good host. Perhaps too good. Donna didn't need that much attention, Rachel thought, unless Evan was getting serious about her. Oh, no. Not another aspiring *artiste* who'd strip him clean, Rachel thought despairingly. She vividly remembered the exotic dancer who'd been a stripper in more ways than one. She'd have to ask Jawbone. Maybe he knew something about Donna.

"Hi, darlin'." Jawbone grinned and hugged her. "How ya doin'?"

"Fine. How about yourself?"

"Pretty good," he said, bobbing his snow white head.

He looked older than his years, thanks to the hard living he'd done for most of his adult life. "You're looking good," she half fibbed. He did too, but then, the last time she'd seen him was in the drunk tank from which she'd rescued him. Like Evan, he was a likable drunk, if that wasn't a contradiction in terms. Neither of them ever turned abusive or violent. Maudlin, sentimental weeping was more their style.

"Do you know anything about Donna?" Rachel asked him.

He shrugged. "She's been around for a while, and she ain't half bad."

"But?"

"She ain't livin', breathin' music. She ain't . . . what you call it? Committed? Yeah, committed."

Jawbone seemed proud of knowing that word, and Rachel repressed a smile. "But do you *know* anything about her?" she persisted.

"Oh. Personal, like?"

"Yes, personal."

Jawbone scratched his head thoughtfully. "Come to think on it, nothin' really. You want more of that stuff?" he asked, indicating her glass. "I'm beginnin' to like club soda, and that worries me some."

Rachel laughed, handing him her glass. "Don't worry about it. It won't make you fat, give you a fatal disease, or bankrupt you."

He grinned sheepishly and left with their glasses.

"You worried about the competition?"

Rachel whirled around. "What?"

"I said, are you worried about the competition?" Blackie repeated, nodding his head toward Evan and Donna.

That's what she thought she'd heard the first time. It didn't make any more sense on hearing it again. She detected undisguised antagonism in his voice. "I'm afraid that once again you've lost me. I've never met a man with whom I communicated less well than I do with you."

"On a certain level we communicate just fine. The physical level. What we're having trouble on is the moral level. You think about that," he advised cryptically, and he left her to join Poco and his wife.

Moral level? There was definitely something wrong with that man. What a shame. He was the most attractive man she'd ever met. Just her luck, Rachel mourned. Why didn't she simply give up? Maybe she wasn't destined to have a man of her own. She had just about come to that conclusion this past year when the miraculous reunion of Laura and Harley, teenage sweethearts who met and married twenty years later, gave her hope.

Still, for some people there might be a second chance, but obviously not for her. She was destined to be a career woman and an advocate for the protection of animals. Thinking of her affectionate menagerie at home, she cheered up. It wasn't such a bad life.

Jawbone returned with two glasses of club soda and handed her one. "Guess what? Blackie asked me to sit in on the recording."

"That's great," Rachel said, happy for him.

"Yeah. After all them years. That Blackie sure is one fine man."

That seemed to be the consensus of opinion. Rachel frowned. Something was out of sync, she thought. When her father joined them, she decided to ask him flat out.

"What do you really think of Blackie?"

Evan flashed her one of his intense looks. "Why do you ask?"

"Don't you dare answer a question with a question," she answered. "I'm on to that old counseling technique."

Evan and Jawbone grinned at each other.

"Well?" Rachel demanded.

"I told you. He's a good man."

"He doesn't strike you as being odd?"

"Not in the least. The female audience at the club adores him."

No doubt. She hadn't meant odd in that way. Evan was called back to the piano, and he and Jawbone wandered off. Rachel didn't particularly like the way Donna draped herself over her father. She knew too little about the woman. Perhaps she should have asked Evan about Donna instead. He would probably tell her that she was a good woman, Rachel thought wryly. What kind of a woman came to a party with one man and threw herself at another? Why didn't Blackie question Donna's morals? Because she'd come with him?

Blackie couldn't keep his eyes off Rachel for any length of time. The dark hair, the delicately-hued skin, the smoky eyes fascinated him. He saw her look annoyed at Evan and Donna and couldn't blame her. The two were definitely flirting. Deep down he rejoiced. If Donna snared Evan . . . It would hurt Rachel, but he'd make her forget she'd ever even heard of Evan Gregory. He knew he could. Even though he would never cause a rift between his friend and Rachel, he would do nothing to stop one either. With a predatory gleam in his eyes he stalked Rachel until he caught up with her.

"Why don't you spend some time with your date? Do you always bring women to a party and abandon them?" Rachel snapped waspishly.

"My date?"

"Donna, the songbird."

"Ah." Rachel seemed to be jealous of Evan's attention to the singer. Blackie didn't like that one bit. He wanted her to be indifferent toward Evan. Perhaps she was just revealing some hurt pride. He hoped so. "Donna isn't my date."

That cheered Rachel up considerably, even though it still left Donna an unknown quantity. "Whose date is she?"

Rachel's voice had lost its waspish sting, Blackie noticed. Curious, that. "She came alone."

"What do you know about her?"

She couldn't leave it alone, and Blackie didn't like that. He glowered at her. "She works as a waitress, and I believe she's trying to get a singing career going."

"Is she married?"

"No. Divorced, I think she said."

"Does she have children?"

"She didn't mention any. Why are you so interested in Donna?"

"Why shouldn't I be? She's obviously interested in Evan," Rachel pointed out.

Damn. It was worse than he'd feared. Rachel wouldn't give up Evan easily. Maybe he'd better remind her how they reacted to each other. He looked around the room and spotted the patio door. "The smoke in here is getting thick. Come." He took her arm firmly and led her out onto the patio.

"It's a nice night," Rachel said, looking at the starry sky.

"Mmm. I missed seeing you at the club," Blackie

said. He had more style than to pounce on her the minute they were alone.

"I had to go to New Jersey on business."

"Demonstrating cosmetics? I can't think of anyone more suitable for the job."

"Thank you, I think."

"It was a compliment. You look so perfectly put together all the time." He reached out to touch her dark, shiny hair.

"You should see me after I give my dog a bath," Rachel said, and she smiled.

"Ah. All those pets who hop onto your bed. I wouldn't mind sharing it with them," Blackie volunteered.

"You might mind. Sometimes Cleo and Callie decide to chase each other on it in the middle of the night." Why were they discussing her bed, she wondered, warmth flooding her body.

"Rachel." Blackie whispered the name against her slightly parted lips a moment before he claimed them in a heady kiss. Rachel clung to him, letting him do what he wanted, enjoying it. His arms gathered her closer. Her fingers tangled in the thick, black hair at his nape. His beard and mustache felt like the silkiness of feline fur against her skin.

Blackie's hands stroked her back, glorying in the satiny feel of her dress. He trailed kisses down her throat as far as the V-neck of the dress allowed.

"Blackie," she whispered.

He raised his head and looked deeply into her gray eyes.

The only thing to escape her tight-feeling throat was a nondescript sound.

"I know how you feel. We kiss, and I hear notes that don't exist."

"Maybe it's just a fluke. Next time we kiss, we might wonder what we thought we felt. It might be a quite ordinary experience."

"Think so, huh? Let's put it to the test." He did. He kissed her repeatedly.

"Ready to admit that there's something special about us?" he demanded.

"Well, yes." For now at least. For a while. She needed to remind herself that, with musicians, nothing lasted but the music. She had to keep that in mind at all times. That way, she prayed, she wouldn't slip and allow herself to create fantasies and expectations. With someone like Blackie there couldn't be any expectations.

"So cautious," he murmured. "Take a chance." His voice was sweetly persuasive.

"And regret it tomorrow?"

"You don't know that you will. Odds are you won't. I can practically guarantee you won't."

"Sure of yourself, aren't you?"

"Of us."

She'd sworn off men in general, hadn't she, and musicians in particular? There were excellent reasons she'd done that, but at the moment they didn't seem to matter. She scarcely remembered them.

"Take a chance," Blackie whispered seductively again.

He feathered kisses over her face, murmuring endearments. "Let's go tell Evan that you're through with him."

Rachel pulled her face back to look at him. "Why would I be through with Evan?"

Blackie's body rocked to a dead stop. "You're not suggesting that you have us both?"

"Why not?" Blackie was not making any sense.

"Why not? Why not?" he yelled. "Dear heaven above, don't you have any sense of decency? Of morality? What is it with you? I can offer you what he can. Maybe more. Do you have such a vested interest in the man?"

Thirty-four years would qualify for that. "Yes, I do. Years and years. He's my daddy."

"Your sugar daddy, you mean. Are you afraid that I can't keep you in perfume and dresses? Man, was I fooled by you. I didn't realize how mercenary you are."

This was too much for Rachel to take in. "Sugar daddy?" she asked, still unable to believe he'd said that.

"Yeah. Let me define it for you: an old man who keeps a young woman by giving her expensive things. Payment for services rendered," Blackie snapped, his voice like steel.

"And you think Evan and I have that kind of relationship?"

"Obviously."

For a moment Rachel was torn between anger and laughter. The anger won out, not only because he refused to believe her, but also because he thought her capable of such duplicity.

"You think I could be out here with you and minutes later go to another man? You think me so unprincipled, so immoral?" Before she knew what she'd done, her palm had connected soundly with his cheek. Rachel turned and ran back into the living room, leaving Blackie standing there, touching the cheek she'd slapped.

Chapter Four

To say that a feather could have knocked him over wasn't claiming too much, Blackie thought.

Joining him on the patio, Jawbone looked at Blackie curiously. "You okay, man?"

"If somebody suffering from foot-in-mouth disease can be okay, then I am, I guess," Blackie said, still stunned. "How long have you known Rachel?"

"Since the day she was born. Evan called me, all excited, from the hospital." Remembering, Jawbone chuckled. "He was standing in front of the nursery, proud as a peacock, telling everybody, 'That's my little girl.' With all that black hair, Rachel was the prettiest thing."

She was still the prettiest thing, only Blackie had a sinking feeling that Rachel wouldn't want to see him. He'd royally screwed up. It hadn't even occurred to him that Evan might really be her father. Why should it, he rationalized, when she called the man by his first name? It wasn't exactly common practice to call a parent by his first name, he thought, aggrieved. That was an open invitation to a man to make a fool of himself.

"You two have an argument?" Jawbone asked.

"What makes you think that?" Blackie inquired, his tone dry.

"There was a storm brewing in them light eyes of hers. Oooeee! She more than once cut her eyes like that at me and Evan when we'd come home at four or five in the mornin', and I never liked it one bit—no, sir. I'd just as soon take a beatin' than have her eyeball me like that." Jawbone shuddered delicately.

"I'm not exactly crazy about it myself. Does she stay mad long?" Blackie asked cautiously.

Jawbone lifted his bony shoulders in an elaborate shrug. "Depends on what you did. You like Rachel?"

The question caught Blackie completely unprepared. He hadn't thought about liking her. He desired her. He knew that for a fact. He also wanted her to like his music, he wanted her to like him, he wanted her to be with him, and he wanted . . . Sweet clashing cymbals. Yes, he liked her. There was no doubt about it. The realization hit him with the force of a poleax.

"Man, you don't look so good. You want me to get you a drink? A glass of water? Some aspirin?"

"Hmm? No, thanks, Jawbone. I just need a breath of fresh air," Blackie said, and he headed for the living room, looking like a man in a trance, his mind a million miles away.

"Huh?" Jawbone looked around, momentarily wondering if he was hallucinating. No, he hadn't had a drink in weeks. He was standing out in the fresh air. Then a knowing look crept into his faded eyes. "It's like that, is it?" he murmured to himself, and he smiled in understanding.

A few miles away, Rachel stormed into her house and slammed the door resoundingly. The cats, hating loud noises, sat up in alarm, whiskers twitching. Piccolo barked a greeting and wagged his tail. The phone rang.

"Hush, Piccolo," she admonished the dog as she picked up the phone. "Hello?" Mumbling sounds assailed her ears. "I'm sorry, but I can't understand you."

"That's because my foot is in my mouth," Blackie said.

"You!"

"Rachel, I'm sorry."

"Well, you can just put your foot back into your mouth, because I'm not listening or talking to you."

"Let me explain, please—"

"Good-bye." Rachel dropped the receiver and refused to answer the phone when it rang again. And again.

Rachel changed into sweatpants and a T-shirt and took Piccolo for a walk. How could Blackie have thought her capable of such despicable behavior? She'd assumed he found her attractive. Ha!

Well, maybe he had, she conceded. But he couldn't possibly like her. Not and think she was so shallow and so immoral.

This was probably a blessing in disguise. She'd

come dangerously close to finding him irresistibly attractive, even though she knew he was a musician.
Dumb, Rachel, dumb, she scolded herself. Yes, this was
for the best, she decided, and she heaved a heartbreak-
ing sigh.

"Any messages?" Rachel asked Peggy the next
morning.

"Yes and no."

"What does that mean?"

"He doesn't leave any messages or tell me his name,
but he keeps calling."

"Who?" Rachel asked with a frown.

"The man with the sexy voice."

Blackie. It had to be. "For him I'm not in," Rachel
ordered, and she swept into her office. So, Blackie was
still trying to apologize. Let him. She wasn't ready to
accept his apology. Eventually she'd have to, because
Evan liked him and worked with him. Not yet, though.
Rachel forced herself to concentrate on her work. At
eleven she buzzed Peggy, and together they finished the
correspondence.

"Your sexy mystery caller? The one with the dyna-
mite voice? He keeps phoning every fifteen minutes,"
Peggy revealed.

"What?" Rachel asked, horrified. "He's tying up the
line that way. This is a business. He can't do that."

"Maybe you'd better take the next call and tell him
that."

"Maybe I'd better," Rachel agreed, her voice grim.

She was all prepared to deal with him sternly, but he didn't stick to his fifteen-minute pattern. Rachel received a number of phone calls during the next hour, so when she heard his voice, she wasn't ready for him. Peggy had been right. Over the phone Blackie's voice was even sexier. Perhaps when she'd been face-to-face with him, his looks had distracted her, and she hadn't noticed the nerve-tingling timbre of his low voice.

"Will you please not call every fifteen minutes?" Rachel requested.

"Why? Will you get into trouble with your boss if I do?"

Not exactly, though it wouldn't do to tell him that. Aloud she said, "This is a business. I can't tie up a line with personal calls."

"Okay, I won't call so often. Will you go to dinner with me?"

"What?" she asked, astonished by his brazen request.

"So that I can apologize properly," he explained.

"I haven't even decided yet if I'm going to accept your apology."

"Not *if*. *When*. You can't walk around forever being angry with me."

"Oh? And why not?" Rachel demanded.

"It would upset Evan. You don't want that, do you?" Blackie asked silkily.

"Don't be so sure about what I will and will not do," she snapped.

"I'm sorry. I'm apologizing again for jumping to conclusions."

"I'm not accepting your apology. Not yet, anyway," she maintained.

Blackie sighed dramatically. "I guess I'll have to live with that. Just remember that it's divine to forgive," he said, and he hung up quickly, sensing an emotional outburst forming at the other end of the line.

Rachel glowered at the phone as if the hapless instrument were responsible for the words flowing through it. "Divine, indeed," she muttered. That man. It wasn't enough that Blackie had upset her private life; now he'd invaded her working world, and that was the one thing she wouldn't tolerate. Resolutely she snapped up a folder from her desk and joined the advertising staff in the conference room.

"What have you got?" Rachel asked Jay.

He flipped the cover off the large sketch pad on the easel and stepped back. While Rachel studied the sketch, Jay polished his glasses.

"I like it. It's good," she said. "What kind of egg are you going to use?"

The question obviously bewildered him. "The kind you buy in a supermarket. What other kinds are there?" Jay asked.

"You apparently don't do the family shopping," Rachel said. "Eggs come in different sizes, from jumbo to small. Let's use a small brown egg. That'll form an even greater contrast between the beautiful, bejeweled egg on the left and the insignificant brown one on the right."

"I've never even seen a brown egg," Jay admitted.

"They're usually in the section with the organic veg-etables. Some people won't eat any other kind. Okay, go ahead and prepare the mock-up. I think this is going to be one of the best ad campaigns we've ever had." Smiling happily, she went back to her office.

In the middle of her desk sat a long, narrow box. The kind florists used. Rachel pushed the intercom button. "Peggy, what's this box doing on my desk?"

"It was delivered for you just a minute ago."

"Who delivered it?"

"Some guy wearing overalls. I signed for it. Shouldn't I have?"

"It's okay," Rachel assured her. She double-checked the name on the box. It was hers. She removed the lid and carefully parted the tissue paper.

"Do you need a vase?" Peggy asked from the doorway.

"Oh, my." Rachel lifted the single, long-stemmed rose. The color shaded from deep pink at the tips of the petals into gold at the base. Rachel inhaled the exqui-site fragrance.

"It's beautiful. What kind is it?" Peggy asked.

Rachel examined the fragrance again. "It's a hybrid tea rose. The name is Tiffany, I think. Now, if we could only capture this scent and transfer it to hard-milled soap."

"Is there a card?" Peggy asked, not bothering to dis-guise her curiosity.

Even though Rachel had a fair idea who'd sent the rose, she reached for the small envelope and ripped it open.

Since I promised not to tie up your phone line, I considered a number of ways to get in touch with you . . . carrier pigeons, singing telegrams, sky-writing airplanes, strolling mariachi players . . . Aren't you glad I settled for a more conservative, traditional method?

In spite of her best efforts, a smile tilted Rachel's lips upward. She read on.

Think about my apology.
Yours, Blackie

"The man with the sexy voice?" Peggy guessed.

"The very same."

"Does the rest of him match the voice?"

"Yes, unfortunately."

"Why unfortunately?"

"Because the combination makes him hard to resist or stay angry with," Rachel explained.

"Why be angry with a gorgeous man? Or, for that matter, why fight the attraction? It's not as if his kind grows on trees, you know. I'll put this beauty into a vase," Peggy said, and she left with the rose and the box.

Rachel looked at the note for a moment and then dropped it into her handbag. She couldn't bring herself to throw it away. With an equal mixture of disgust and guilt she muttered, "I'm getting sentimental in my old age." To make up for this descent into mawkishness, she attacked the work on her desk with the fervor of the devil recruiting souls.

Consequently, it was almost nine o'clock when she unlocked the front door of her house. She heard the phone ring and hoped whoever was on the other end was patient. The caller was. It was still ringing when Rachel rushed into the kitchen and dumped the two bags of groceries and her purse onto the counter.

Careful not to step on any members of her menagerie, who milled around her legs, she grabbed the phone. "Hello?"

"Finally. I've been worried. Wondered if I should send out a search party for you."

Blackie.

"I worked late, and then I had to stop at the grocery store. Why I'm explaining this to you, I don't know. I still don't want to talk to you, you rat."

At least she hadn't been out with another man, Blackie thought, and a heavy load of worry dropped from his soul. "I don't mean to harass you, but I do want to see you again. When are you coming to the club next?"

"I don't know yet. Every time I think about what sort of woman you thought I was, I get angry all over again."

"It's good to let the anger out. Healthy. And the sooner you purge it from your system, the better. So, go on, call me names or whatever it takes," Blackie offered eagerly.

"Don't patronize me with glib pop psychology," Rachel snapped. "I haven't forgiven you yet."

Blackie winced. The sound of a phone being hung up

forcefully wasn't pleasant. He hadn't expected her to be ready to fall into his arms, though that's what he dreamed about, hoped, and prayed for. It would take time, and that was the problem. It had taken him thirty-six years to find Rachel, and that was long enough. He didn't have time to play foolish games.

He'd have to come up with something special to win her pardon, Blackie realized. He stroked his beard, thinking. A car drove past. The blast of music from its radio gave him the glimmering of an idea. With a faint grin he sprinted across the street and entered the club.

The next day another rose arrived. And the next and every day thereafter. On the seventh day Rachel decided that enough was enough. Not that she didn't enjoy the roses, or that deep down she wasn't pleased by the attention, but this romantic gesture was costing Blackie a small fortune, a fortune he probably didn't have. He might be skipping meals or living on peanut butter sandwiches or on rice and sardines—Jawbone's mainstay when he'd been down and out, and Rachel had been too young to help him.

The problem, Rachel discovered, was that she had no idea where Blackie lived. The telephone directory listed a number of Madigans but none with a first name sounding even remotely like Blackie. That obviously was a nickname. Most musicians had one. Evan should know where she could reach Blackie. Her father was at home and delighted to hear from her.

"I've missed you at the club," Evan said. "Have you been real busy at work?

"Sort of. How's the music going?"

"Great. Tomorrow's our first session in the recording studio."

"How exciting. Are you nervous?"

"A little."

"How can I get a hold of Blackie?" Rachel prayed that her voice sounded calm and nonchalant.

"Have you stopped being mad at him?"

"What do you know about that?" Rachel asked, surprised.

"Not much, except Blackie asked me if you held a grudge."

"What did you say?"

"Only for a while. Eventually you get over it." When Rachel didn't say anything, Evan added, "Well, it's true. You always forgave me. And Jawbone."

True. She couldn't stay angry long. At least not with Evan or Jawbone. Blackie, however, was another matter. He could hurt her on an entirely different, more intense level. "Do you have a phone number for Blackie?"

"Just a minute. I've got it here somewhere. He said I could leave a message there for him."

So, Blackie didn't have a phone. Even though Rachel wasn't that familiar with the Chicago area yet, she was sure the city had its seamier neighborhoods. Blackie probably had a room in one of the cheap boarding houses located in such areas.

The number Evan gave her was that of a cafe patronized by jazz musicians. The proprietor, an ex-musician, acted as secretary, den mother, and father confessor, Evan told her.

Remembering Blackie's lack of funds and his worn sneakers, Rachel asked casually, "Do you think Blackie's particularly hard up just now?"

"I have a hunch Blackie can take care of himself. He's not one of your strays to be taken home with you," Evan warned.

Stung, Rachel replied a little huffily, "I have no intention of taking him home with me."

"That's good, because I suspect he's not the kind who takes easily to being domesticated," Evan cautioned.

No, Blackie didn't seem to be the pipe-and-slippers type, she thought after she hung up. What type was he? There was something wild and passionate in his music, and sometimes a hint of pain and forlornness sneaked in. He was a loyal friend and obviously lived by a code of ethics. She liked that, liked it a lot. He was committed to his music, and even though she liked that too, she knew that Blackie would never be that committed to anything or anyone else. She must not forget this dispiriting fact.

She would never be first in his life. Rachel knew that. Did she want to—could she be satisfied with—playing the proverbial second fiddle? She remembered his kisses, remembered the strength of his arms, and tingling warmth flowed through her body. With a man like Blackie, being second in importance would be more exciting than being first with most other men.

With a start Rachel realized the dangerous direction her thoughts were taking. She would have to get a hold of herself. The last thing she needed was to become involved with a musician. A jazz musician. A sax man. She groaned and pressed the open palm of one hand against her forehead. Had she taken leave of her senses? "Idiot," she hissed. "Haven't you learned anything from your past mistakes?" She jerked the phone closer and dialed the cafe's number.

"I'd like to leave a message for Blackie Madigan, please."

"Just a sec," the man replied. "Go ahead."

"Tell Mr. Madigan I absolutely forbid him to send me any more roses. He'll know who left the message. Thank you." That had been her best lady-of-the-manor voice, Rachel thought, pleased. The man wouldn't fail to inform Blackie of the tone in which the message had been delivered. That should clue him in and stop him from wasting money on her.

It did.

No rose was delivered at the usual time the next day. Though she was pleased by Blackie's sensible decision, deep down Rachel experienced a twinge of regret. She squelched it promptly and turned her attention to her work, grateful she could escape into it completely. Well, almost completely. From time to time throughout the day a thought or two strayed in his direction.

They hadn't seen each other for over a week. Surely that was long enough to dampen the dangerous attraction she'd felt for him. She was strong enough for a visit to

The Blues in the Night, she decided. Unless she was traveling on business, she never let so much time elapse without seeing Evan. Yes, she'd go to the club that evening. Once she made that decision, a buoyant feeling coursed through her and stayed with her the rest of the day.

She was actually nervous, she discovered when she parked her car behind the club. Which was ridiculous, she told herself. She could leave any time she wanted. She didn't even have to talk to Blackie. Keeping that in mind, she paid the cover charge at the door and went in.

Although Rachel had tried to time her arrival to coincide with the beginning of a new set, she had miscalculated. That wasn't difficult to do. No two sets played were exactly the same length, because the improvisations varied.

Why did it have to be Blackie her eyes focused on first? He stood in profile to her, giving her a chance to admire the fine shape of his head, the close-cropped beard that she knew was silken soft. Her gaze sank to his muscular arms, bare in a short-sleeved shirt, and to the lean length of his legs. Rachel swallowed and wondered if coming to the club had been a mistake.

Nonsense, she told herself. So he was as handsome as Lucifer; she had met handsome men before. She could handle it. Seeing an unoccupied table at the back, she made a beeline for it. Evan saw her and waved. She waved back. When Jawbone spotted her, he rushed to join her.

"Are you sitting in tonight?" she asked him excitedly.

"Sure am, darlin'."

His eyes were suspiciously bright, and the familiar panic hit her. "Jawbone, are you on something?"

"Dang. You're the most suspicious female I ever met," he said, feigning a hurt expression. But his good mood was too intense. He grinned. "I'm flying' high on the music, darlin'. Today we recorded 'Relaxin' at Camarillo,' and it was awesome."

"Are you going to record any other Charlie Parker tunes?" she asked.

"Blackie said we'd do 'Yardbird Suite'. And then some music he's composed in honor of Bird. That Blackie is one talented guy. Well, I see we're getting ready to play. Enjoy, darlin'."

"I will."

Blackie turned, and she thought he recognized her, but she couldn't be sure. The lighting was dim, and she was sitting at the very back of the club. He'd been talking to a woman. A slender, attractive redhead. A sharp jab of jealousy knifed through her.

She couldn't believe she was jealous. Hadn't she told herself countless times that she would be better off without him? Blackie was a musician, a sax man, and that by definition made him fickle, footloose, and impecunious. She had that on the best authority: her firsthand experience. Rachel crossed her arms over her chest with steely determination to resist Blackie Madigan.

So, she'd come. Finally. Blackie realized she'd come because of Evan, but that didn't matter. She was there. That gave him a chance. He picked up his saxophone.

"Evan, how do you feel about doing a Parker number?" Blackie asked offhandedly.

Evan arched an eyebrow. "Any special reason for that?"

Blackie grinned. "There might be."

"Thought so," Evan said, looking in Rachel's direction.

He would play for her as he had never played before, Blackie vowed. His horn would tell her how much he wanted her, how much he needed her. In his music he never lied. He couldn't, even if he wanted to. Rachel would know that, just as she would understand the message of his horn. *All right, Rachel honey, this is for you.*

From the first note she was mesmerized. Either the sextet played unusually well that evening, or it simply seemed so to her because she hadn't heard them for a while. Either way, the music entrapped her. Rachel tried to fight the fatal pull but lost. Everything else paled into insignificance.

Blackie's solos were played with an unabashed intensity and passionate abandon that caused her scalp to tighten and goose bumps to rise up on her skin. He became one with the music, a living flame, caressing her, seducing her, and Rachel knew with unmistakable clarity and certainty that if she didn't leave right then, she would be lost. As quietly and unobtrusively as she could, she walked out of the club.

Blackie saw her leave, and for a moment his face darkened. Then the import of her flight hit him, and a gleeful light danced in his eyes. Rachel had understood the message of his music—there was no doubt about that—and it had frightened her. So it should. The intensity of his feelings for her shocked him a little too. But it was something they would have to accept, for it was inescapable. She hadn't accepted that yet, but she would. Rachel was only beginning to realize that, and that was why she had fled.

Blackie smiled a knowing, secretive smile and raised the horn to his lips.

Chapter Five

Pressing her face into one pillow and covering her head with another, Rachel tried to shut out the sounds. It didn't work. Blackie's music had sunk deep roots into her brain. She couldn't turn it off. Impatiently she flung the pillow from her head, flipped over, and stared at the ceiling. At the foot of the bed the cats stirred, upset by her restlessness.

"Blast you, Blackie Madigan!" she cried out. He'd known exactly what he was doing to her. It had been a calculated assault on her senses. The frightening part was that it had almost worked. If she'd stayed . . .

"Svengali Madigan," she muttered, and she pounded the pillow, trying to get comfortable. It was no use.

Sighing, she got out of bed and unrolled her exercise mat. She sat upright, knees bent, ankles crossed, hands resting on her knees in the Jnana Mudra position. Starting with a series of deep-breathing exercises, she could feel herself relax. Hatha yoga did that for her. By the time she was through with the slow, tension-relieving stretching exercises, she knew she was ready to go into the deep-relaxation pose and into sleep.

At Athena the next day, Rachel paced. She'd taken off the jacket of her beige ensemble. The only jewelry she wore were large gold hoop earrings, which she fingered absentmindedly.

Quality. Originality. Those had to be the key concepts in the giveaway, which had to be something radically different from the usual packets of miniature bottles of lotion and cologne. But what? Passing the ornate French mirror on the wall, Rachel caught sight of her reflection. Then she did a classic double take and turned back.

Original. Every *woman* was original. That was it. Rachel practically ran out of her office and knocked on Laura's door. Barely waiting for the "Come in," she burst into the room.

"I've got it! I've got the slogan for the Amour giveaway."

Seeing her enthusiasm, she invited, "Tell me about it." A warm smile lit Laura's features.

"The key word is *original.* It just came to me as I saw my reflection in the mirror. I'm an original. So are you. So is every woman. Amour's an original. The slogan could be 'One original deserves another—Amour and You.' A mirror somehow has to be part of the giveaway. What do you think?"

Laura got up out of her chair. "I think that's a great slogan," she said enthusiastically. "Why don't we feature the mirror itself as the giveaway? A silver-plated hand mirror. It could be the first part of a dresser set. We could bring out the brush and the comb at two- or three-month intervals."

"The handle and the frame of the mirror could be fluted and decorated with romantic scrolls. I can just see it. It'll be so elegant. We'll blow Exotica's cheap imitation right out of the water." Rachel's eyes danced with excitement.

"Maybe we could add a tray. Let's see. It's early May. We could be ready with the mirror by late July. Have the brush out in September, the comb in November, and the tray by Christmas."

"The set would make a great Christmas gift," Rachel said. Then the enormity of the undertaking hit her.

"You look as if somebody just burst your bubble. What's the matter? I know this will be a sixteen-hour-a-day type of undertaking, but we can do it. We've done it before."

"I know we can do it. I was thinking of Henry."

A little of the enthusiasm drained out of Laura too. "Yes. There's Henry to contend with."

"This will cost us a fortune. Henry is going to have kittens when he hears about it. Maybe we'd better have the paramedics standing by when we tell him," Rachel joked.

"Maybe it won't be so bad if we make this a bit more attractive to Henry. Listen. Suppose we don't give the mirror away but make it available at a reasonable price," Laura said.

Rachel caught up the thread of Laura's thinking. "Hmm. Something like, buy ten dollars' worth of Athena quality cosmetics, and you get this elegant mirror for x number of dollars."

"Exactly. Because they're buying the cosmetics, we could let them have the mirror for what it'll cost us."

"Great. Henry will go for it, because we'll still make a profit," Rachel agreed.

"I think I know just the artist to design the dresser set. I'll call her today."

"Fine. I'll get on with my end of the campaign." Rachel rushed back to her office, excitement bubbling through her like effervescent wine. She turned on the computer to study their inventory. If they were going to offer the first package in two and a half months, they needed a big inventory of their less expensive items. Rachel worked steadily, losing track of time until Peggy interrupted her.

"Don't forget that you have to pick up your cat at the clinic," Peggy said from the doorway.

Without prying her gaze from the monitor, Rachel said, "Thanks for reminding me, but that's not till six o'clock."

"Since it's five-thirty already, that doesn't leave you much time."

Rachel looked at Peggy, noting that she was dressed to leave for the day. "Good grief. What happened to the afternoon?"

Peggy smiled. "You're as bad as Laura when you get started on something. Good night."

"Good night." Rachel made a few more notes before she shut the computer down. Then she telephoned the clinic, assuring them that she was on her way.

This was the first time she'd seen Trio without the plastic collar around his neck that had kept him from ripping the stitches out of the stump that was left of his hind leg. They placed the black-and-white cat in a cage for the trip to his new home. Rachel spoke in a low, soothing voice to the frightened animal. He had every reason to be afraid. The past weeks had been terrifying and traumatic. Since she didn't want to add to his fears, she'd have to introduce Trio slowly to the menagerie at home.

Leaving him in the car, Rachel spent a few minutes with her animals. Piccolo loved going outside, so she let him into the small, fenced backyard. Trio would be most wary of the dog, and Rachel thought it best to let them get acquainted last. The girls reacted as expected. They circled the cage, sniffing cautiously. When Trio stood up, Cleo hissed and, retreating a couple of steps, sat in her tortoiseshell, dignified beauty and feigned indifference. Callie, the fearless, assertive, daintily pretty calico, sat nose to nose with the newcomer, eyeing him with an unblinking topaz stare. There'd be a few territorial disputes, but they'd accept him. Rachel smiled, relieved.

When the doorbell rang, she frowned. She wasn't

expecting anyone, least of all the deliveryman on her front steps. For one crazy moment she hoped it would be a rose sent by Blackie. It wasn't. She signed for the manila envelope. Curiosity hurried her back to the kitchen for a knife to open the envelope. She extracted two pieces of sheet music. The title on the top sheet read, "Blackie's Apology to Rachel."

Smiling, she shook her head. Leave it to Blackie to come up with an unusual, creative way to apologize. If only she could read the notes that covered the pages. Never having learned to read music, she'd have to wait and have Evan play the piece for her. Eagerly she dialed his number and let the phone ring a dozen times. Blast. She'd have to wait.

Rachel tacked the sheets to the message board in her kitchen, and, despite her best efforts, all evening long her gaze kept straying to the score. She was dying to hear that black-hearted Svengali's apology.

Evan's phone kept ringing uselessly all evening. Rachel knew the sextet wasn't playing at the club that evening, so where was her father?

After supper she let Piccolo back into the house. He loped good-naturedly toward the cage and nosed it curiously. When he came too close, Trio arched his back and hissed. Warned off, the dog kept a respectful distance.

Rachel spread newspapers on the floor beneath the living room window, donned rubber gloves, and proceeded to strip the ugly dark paint off the wooden frame. It was a messy job, but if it wasn't done properly, it would create an even greater mess when she re-painted. It was a case of "If you want it done right, do it yourself."

At ten-thirty she carried Trio to the laundry room, where she'd fixed a bed for him. He seemed to be glad to get out of his cage. She bathed, selected an outfit for the next day, and went to bed.

Rachel wondered where Blackie was, what he was doing, if he was playing that seductive instrument of his somewhere. She was thinking of him so intently that she could hear his music as if he were right there playing for her. The power of the imagination was unbeliev-able, she thought drowsily. Then her eyes flew open, and she shot out of bed as if catapulted. Peering down from her open bedroom window, she saw Blackie.

"The power of imagination, my foot," she muttered. He was standing on her stoop, serenading her. She gaped at him disbelievingly. The rolling sax notes floated up to her pleadingly, sweetly, intoxicatingly.

"Rachel, come out, come out wherever you are," Blackie chanted seductively. "I won't leave until you do."

"Blackie, you're crazy. You'll wake up the entire neighborhood," Rachel called down to him.

He looked up, and she thought he was smiling. "Then come down and talk to me." He raised the horn and let loose a full, rich glissando.

"Stop that," Rachel ordered, knowing her protest was futile. She grabbed her robe, slipped it over her head, and zipped it with unsteady fingers. She ran downstairs and unlocked the front door.

"Come in before the neighbors call the police," she hissed, and she pulled him inside by one arm.

"My, my. Such unseemly haste to get me into your house. Are you planning to kiss me right here in the vestibule?" he asked, arching an eyebrow teasingly.

"You should live so long," she muttered darkly as she closed the door behind him.

Piccolo barked, sniffed Blackie's chinos, and walked off, satisfied.

"Some guard dog you are," Rachel said, but the disapproval slid off Piccolo's back like water off a duck.

"Don't you know I have a way with creatures having silky hair?" Blackie reached out and touched Rachel's shiny, dark hair.

"Stop that," she said, slapping at his hand. "I'm still mad at you." *Or trying to be,* she added silently.

"Then I'll play my apology again."

Before she could stop him, the sweet melody reached out to her, wooing her shamelessly, intensely. Well, she'd been dying to hear the composition all evening, hadn't she? She might as well enjoy it. But not too much, she told herself sternly.

"That's my apology expressed in the medium I know best—music." The azure eyes studied her intently.

"It's the most beautiful apology I've ever received," she managed at last.

Blackie took a step towards her.

"But that's all," she said, raising a hand, stopping him. "Nothing else has changed. You're still a jazz musician, a horn man."

That stopped him cold. "What's wrong with playing the horn? As for being a jazzman, so is your father."

"Precisely."

Blackie frowned. "I don't understand."

"Music always comes first with people like you, and jazz men are fickle, footloose, and impecunious."

A grin split that seductive mouth of his. "I dare you to repeat that in double time."

"Oh, no," Rachel groaned. "Tell me you're not one of those infuriating people who refuses to argue. I hate it when I'm spoiling for a good fight, and all my opponent does is humor me."

"Okay, I won't tell you that." Blackie's face turned serious. "You and I need to discuss your conception of jazz musicians. Offer me a cup of coffee, Rachel."

She saw his determined expression and gave up all thoughts of objecting. "Okay. But not coffee. It's too late at night to load your system with caffeine." She started toward the kitchen, and Blackie followed.

"Bossy, aren't you?" he asked with a grin.

Rachel didn't deign to answer that. "You have your choice of chamomile or hibiscus tea. Neither contains caffeine."

"Herb tea?" He made it sound like something the cat had dragged in.

"It's good for you. Soothing."

"If you say so. You choose, please."

Rachel turned to the stove so that he couldn't see her amused expression. She put the teakettle on. She rinsed the teapot with hot water to warm it. When the water came to a boil, she steeped the tea bags. "Hand me two mugs from the cupboard behind you, please."

She filled them and carried them to the table by the window. When he looked apprehensively at his mug, she said, "It's fragrant and really quite tasty. I won't offer you sugar, but if you want to sweeten it with honey, I'll get it for you."

"Oh. Well, I suppose I'm sweet enough," Blackie joked.

"I doubt that." *Sweet* was not an adjective that came to mind when she thought about Blackie. *Dangerous, seductive,* and *sexy* were some of the terms she associated with him.

"So, I'm not sweet, and being a jazzman by your definition makes me also fickle, footloose, and . . . What was the third thing? Ah, yes. Impecunious. And you don't like my saxophone. Looks like I've got my work cut out for me, trying to improve my image with you." He slouched back in the kitchen chair, crossing his long legs at the ankles.

He looked at ease in her kitchen, she thought. "You don't seem to be too worried about your image, and I didn't say I don't like your saxophone," Rachel protested.

"But you implied that there was something bothering you about the horn," he insisted.

Didn't he hear how voluptuously sensuous its sound was? Was she the only one who felt that? "I like the saxophone. Its tone is . . . mesmerizing . . . spellbinding. That makes it dangerous." She probably shouldn't have admitted that. She *knew* she shouldn't have when she looked into his eyes. Blackie sat up in the chair. Leaning forward he brought his body closer to her, and she tensed.

"What gave you the low opinion you have of jazz musicians?" he demanded.

"Experience."

His eyes searched her face. "I realize that life with your father couldn't have always been easy, but there's more to it, isn't there?"

"Yes."

Blackie reached for her hand and held it protectively. "Tell me about it, please."

His voice was low, compelling, not unlike the horn he played. "All right. It's no secret. When I was very young, I married a saxophone player. It didn't work out."

"Ah. Was he fickle?"

"Yes."

"The fool." Blackie raised her hand to his lips and kissed her palm.

Rachel felt that kiss in every nerve ending of her body.

"Footloose? Was he that too?"

"Yes. He couldn't settle down." Undomesticated, like the man holding her hand.

"And he was always broke?"

"Mmm. Money ran through his fingers like water. And when I found out that he really liked his liquor, that did it. I could see myself a few years down the road being just as miserable as my mother was." Rachel's shudder underscored her words.

He needed to set her straight on that point. "Rachel,

what you see me drink at the club when I'm working is plain ginger ale. I told you that. I couldn't drink alcohol and still play. Nobody can."

"I wondered about that. When Evan drinks and tries to play, his fingers somehow land between the keys."

"Let me tell you something about me. Yes, I am a jazz musician, and, yes, I am a sax player, but I'm not fickle, especially not now at the advanced age of thirty-six."

His grin made him look younger, and with the vitality that emanated from him, age was hardly one of his problems.

"And I'm not footloose. I intend to stick around here as long as I can get gigs."

"As good as you are, that shouldn't be difficult."

"Thank you. At least you like my music, even if you don't like musicians. That brings me to the impoverished part. True, most of us don't earn a lot playing in clubs, but few of us are actually starving."

"Then you're not living on rice and sardines?"

"That's a revolting combination!" he exclaimed.

Seeing the expression of distaste on his handsome face, Rachel chuckled. "It's nutritious and cheap. It's Jawbone's mainstay when he's down on his luck. I suppose peanut butter is more to your liking."

"Sure is." He could say that truthfully, even though he hadn't eaten any in years. He made a mental note to buy a jar, so he'd have it on hand when he invited her to his loft. And he would do his damnedest to persuade her, sweet-talk her. Not yet, of course. She was as skittish as that pretty mare he'd bought in early spring. Blossom was now actually glad to see him when he went to his farm. Someday Rachel would be too.

"What are you thinking? Or shouldn't I ask?"

He smiled enigmatically. "Going back to your objections to musicians, I think I've refuted them one by one. You shouldn't lump me into some general category you've formed," he chided gently. "Poco is a family man, and so is Slim, our bass player."

"Exceptions to the rule," Rachel maintained.

"I see I'm going to have to prove myself to you, and that's okay." Blackie suffered a momentary pang of guilt. He hadn't exactly lied about not having much money. It was more a case of omitting part of the truth. He could still rectify his sin of omission, but he didn't want to. For once in his life he had a chance to win the woman he wanted strictly by who he was as a man, not by what he owned or could give her. The prospect was too heady, too enticing, to give up.

The voice of his conscience nagged him, demanding to know how he would explain his wealth to Rachel later, but he dismissed it. He would think of something when the time came.

Rachel took a round tin from a cupboard and brought it to the table.

Blackie studied the kitchen. It was old. The linoleum was worn. The old-fashioned counter and woodwork needed to be painted, and some of the panes were missing from the glass-fronted cabinet doors.

Rachel caught him looking at the kitchen speculatively. "The place needs a lot of work. I've started to strip the paint off the living room windows, but it's slow work."

Hard work too, Blackie reflected, and he found himself wishing he could help her. Unless he found a way to add a few hours to the day, there was no way he could. Of course, he could hire someone to do it for her, but that would shoot his cover as a poor musician. He didn't want to risk that. Not yet, at least.

Rachel opened the tin. "Would you like a cookie?"

"Love one. I'd have thought they'd be on your list of nutritionally worthless foods," he said teasingly. He took a bite.

"Not these. They're special."

"I'll say they are. They're good."

Rachel smiled at his surprised expression. "Nutritious foods don't have to taste bad."

"You know what? You're good for me." He claimed one of her hands and intertwined their fingers.

She liked his holding her hand, but it was potentially dangerous, especially when he looked at her so intently. To defuse a possibly dangerous situation, she said, "I only use natural, unrefined ingredients in my cookies. Not even the raisins and dried apricots are treated with chemicals."

"Homemade cookies," he murmured. He shook his head, bemused. "I haven't had any in . . . years. The disadvantages of being a bachelor, I guess."

"Have you ever been tempted to change your single status?"

"Once. Briefly. Fortunately I came to my senses before I gave in to temptation."

For some inexplicable reason his answer depressed her. Commitment wasn't a priority with him. Except to his music. She'd known that already, so why should this confirmation dampen her mood?

"How about you? Have you thought about marrying again?"

Rachel shrugged. "Sure, I've thought about it, but I never met a man who seemed suitable husband material."

"And what makes a man suitable?" he asked, leaning toward her expectantly.

"A number of things. Like his willingness to commit himself to one woman. Wanting to share, to care. The ability to be faithful. Domesticated things like that. To you that probably sounds deadly boring."

"No. Just domestic."

"The way you say that, it amounts to the same thing," Rachel maintained.

"Not at all," he insisted. "There's something comforting, something appealing in how you describe a relationship. I've never thought of marriage in those terms."

"What did you think marriage would be like?" Rachel was nerve-tinglingly conscious of the pressure of his fingers against hers, of his thumb moving over her hand in a slow, sensuous semicircle.

"From what I've seen from the sidelines, fidelity and caring aren't the dominant ingredients of modern marriage."

"Perhaps not, but they ought to be."

"You're right. Why else bother?"

How had they gotten to the topic of marriage, Rachel wondered. Sitting at her kitchen table in the middle of the night, it wasn't the best choice of topics. "Were you in the studio today?" she asked.

"Uh-huh. Had a real good session. Evan was great."

"I tried getting a hold of him all evening but couldn't."

"He was taking Donna to dinner."

"Oh?"

"Is that a pleased 'oh'?"

"Truthfully? I don't know yet. It'll depend on whether she's good for him or not."

"I told you already that you're good for me. Am I good for you?"

Rachel tried to pull her hand free, but Blackie wouldn't let her. He raised it to his cheek. The silken hair of his beard felt like a fine pelt against her skin. The tempting gesture evoked immense tactile pleasure.

"No answer?" he asked, his rich voice softly insistent.

"Truthfully? I rather doubt it, but I'm not sure."

"Ah, Rachel of the many doubts and prejudices against musicians," he murmured. He moved her palm against his mouth and kissed it. "Well, I have no doubts, but you keep an open mind for now. One of these days you'll see that I'm good for you." He released her hand. "Walk me to the door."

Rachel thought her palm couldn't feel hotter if he'd branded it. Her legs felt wobbly, but she managed to walk to the front door beside him. He picked up his horn. For a moment she thought he was going to kiss her, but he changed his mind.

"Sleep well," he murmured.

"Thanks. You too."

Rachel watched him saunter down the steps, the horn casually slung over his shoulder. She watched his tall figure until darkness hid it from her eyes.

Chapter Six

"Then it's settled. We'll use a small, oval, silver-plated hand mirror with the inscription curved over the upper arc: *One original deserves another–Amour and You.* Any questions?" Laura looked around the conference table. "Henry?"

He was hunched over his calculator, fingers flying over the keys. "I've triple-checked the figures. We'll make a profit, but it's a small one," he pointed out. "Smaller than usual." A slightly accusing tone underscored his words.

"I'm turning the project over to Rachel. The meeting's adjourned," Laura announced.

Laura and Rachel waited for the others to file out ahead of them.

"What's the matter?" Laura asked. "I know you well enough to be sure it isn't business that's worrying you."

"That's true. I have a date." Rachel stopped and shook

her head. "This is ridiculous. You have a date when you're sixteen. At thirty-four I should be able to think of a better word," she complained.

Laura's expression was sympathetic. "I went through the same thing. Only I was thirty-eight, and that made it even worse."

"If I say I have an engagement, that sounds like a business meeting," Rachel said. "*Rendezvous* has the flavor of intrigue or espionage. You know, carnation in the lapel, the *Tribune* folded to the editorial page, stuff like that."

Laura smiled. "How about *tryst*?" she suggested.

"Ye gads! That sounds like a clandestine meeting between a portly, respectable Victorian gentleman wearing a Prince Albert coat and a young shopgirl in a second-rate London hotel."

The women looked at each other and burst into laughter.

"*Date* it is," Rachel conceded, resigned.

"So? In the years I've known you, you've had lots of dates. What makes this one different? Or is it the future possibilities that make it better or worse?" Laura asked.

"You guessed it," Rachel admitted and sighed. "Sometimes I think Blackie could be everything I've ever wanted. Then common sense rears its mundane little head, and I'm convinced that a liaison with this man would be as destructive as the volcanic eruption on Krakatoa."

"What is it about him that makes him so dangerous?"

"You're not going to believe it," Rachel said. Taking a deep breath, she blurted out, "He's a musician."

Laura's dark eyes widened. "Did I hear you right? A musician?" She paused, taking in this unexpected piece of information. "Tell me he's with the symphony," she pleaded.

"Don't I wish! What I wouldn't give if he sat with those tailcoated, bow-tied, conservative members of the wind section, or even the brasses, and performed Mahler and Schubert."

Laura, knowing about Rachel's unhappy marriage to a jazz musician, prepared herself mentally. "So?" she prompted.

"He's a jazzman." Seeing Laura's stunned expression, Rachel warned, "Wait. It gets worse. He plays alto sax."

Laura sank back down into her chair, utterly stunned.

Rachel slumped down on the other side of the table and cradled her face in the palms of her hands.

"All those years ago, when you were so heartbroken, and all the times since then, you swore you'd never . . ." Laura's words trailed off.

"I know what I swore." Rachel groaned. "I swore I'd never get within ten feet of a sax man. And if I did, you were supposed to hit me over the head with a two-by-four to bring me to my senses."

"Why do I get the feeling it's too late for that?"

"Don't say that, please."

"Can I infer that this one's different? You've resisted all other musicians over the years."

Sighing, Rachel agreed. "This one's different. There's something about him that sets him apart. He takes charge of things, and he gets them done. For example, he got a recording contract for the sextet and redesigned a studio to fit their needs. Evan says Blackie's reliable."

"But?" Laura waited to hear Rachel's observations.

"He's as attractive as Lucifer and plays to make the angels weep. I'm sure women fall all over him. I'm equally sure that all he'll ever offer a woman is a wild, brief, fantastic affair before he moves on to the next liaison. Good grief! Do I need or want that?" Rachel asked, agonized. "Is it worth the pain?"

Laura shook her head regretfully. "I don't know. Only you can decide that. Maybe you're wrong about him. From what you've said, he seems to have some business acumen, so maybe he's also more responsible in other areas of his life. Anyway, this is just one date. Right?"

"Right. Indian food at eight."

"Remember what you told me when I was nervous about meeting Harley?"

"No. Refresh my memory."

"Let's see. Something like, 'Wear a pretty dress and a cloud of perfume, and have a good time.' It was good advice."

Rachel returned Laura's grin. "Yeah. I think you're right. I worry too much about things that might never happen."

A few miles from Athena's headquarters Blackie sat in a conference room similar to the one Rachel had just left. Anyone watching him would have thought he was listening attentively and taking notes from time to time.

But he had scanned the report before the meeting, so he allowed his thoughts to drift.

As for taking notes, the serious-looking, three-piece-suit men around the long table would be shocked if they could see the inside of his folder. Rachel's name was written in different scripts, along with musical notes that translated her name into a melody.

After a week of telephoning her, of threatening to serenade her nightly, he'd finally persuaded Rachel to go out to dinner with him. He suppressed a smile when he recalled her diplomatic efforts to go easy on his supposedly lean bank account. His last-minute inspired suggestion—an Indian restaurant, where the food was inexpensive because they served no liquor and thus didn't have to buy the prohibitive liquor license—forestalled her offer of going Dutch. Blackie thought of himself as liberal and enlightened, but he balked at having the woman he dated pay for her own dinner. It just didn't seem right.

". . . what do you think, Blackstone?"

Hastily Blackie rallied his wits. "Yes, if no one has anything else to add, we'll adopt this resolution." Everyone around the table agreed, and Blackie adjourned the meeting.

"Why do I get the feeling that only half of you was present today?" Ben asked.

"I wouldn't know," Blackie answered, but he didn't look at his brother.

"Anyway, do me a favor and look at your latest acquisitions carefully."

"Why? Is something wrong? I glanced at the figures, and they seemed okay."

"Sure. But do you want to diversify that much? I mean, what do you know about the cosmetics business or wine production?"

His mind on the evening ahead, Blackie dismissed his brother's points with a vague promise that he'd study the latest acquisitions of Obsidian International at some future date.

Rachel still couldn't believe she'd actually agreed to go out to dinner with Blackie. Had she lost her mind? But it was to late to call him, even if he'd had a phone.

Looking through her wardrobe, she selected a silk dress with a swingy skirt and a modest petal collar, which struck just the right note between formal and informal. Probably because Amour had been in her thoughts all day, she reached for it and applied it to her wrists and neck. On impulse she also misted her hair with it.

And that was the first thing Blackie noticed. "You smell good," he murmured, bending down to inhale the scent on her hair. He leaned closer. Rachel could feel his warm breath against her ear, her throat, and she stood very still. She focused her eyes on the claw feet of the umbrella stand beside the front door to keep from swaying. If she moved just half an inch, their faces would touch, and she was afraid she might do something as foolish as rub her cheek against his down-soft beard. *Pull yourself together, girl.*

"It's called Amour," she said, her voice faint.

"Very appropriate," he murmured.

Why didn't he move back, Rachel wondered a little desperately. She would, but her legs seemed to be paralyzed. "Our arch competitor is coming out with a cheap imitation. The barracudas!" she heard herself say.

"Oh? Is your company going to sue?"

Rachel could feel his lips against her hair. Sue whom, she wondered, dazed. A car horn broke through the sweet languor. She jerked away from him.

"Our cab is waiting," Blackie explained. "My car is in the shop. Something's wrong with the carburetor." That was true. The Porsche was in the shop for its annual checkup, but even if it hadn't been, Blackie couldn't have used it without raising all sorts of questions in Rachel's already wary mind.

"I have a car. We could take that," Rachel offered.

"No. The restaurant is only a few blocks away. That's the good thing about Chicago. Restaurants everywhere."

"Well, if you're sure." Rachel picked up her clutch and preceded Blackie out the front door.

They didn't talk in the cab. Rachel glanced at Blackie. This was the first time she'd seen him wear a tie and a blazer. He'd exchanged his worn sneakers for black leather loafers. He looked good, but then, he always looked good to her.

When they reached the restaurant, Blackie reached into the back pocket of his slacks and frowned. He never carried much cash, but he thought he'd stuffed some bills into that pocket. He checked the blazer's inner pocket but touched only the plastic of his charge cards. Damn. This was embarrassing.

Seeing his dilemma, Rachel wordlessly handed him a ten-dollar bill.

Blackie flashed her an embarrassed but grateful look and paid the cabby. "Thank you," he murmured. Damn. He'd just reinforced her idea that jazz musicians couldn't handle money. How could he have been so careless as to leave the cash on his dresser? As they walked up the steps to the restaurant, Blackie saw the list of credit cards accepted and felt relieved. "Don't worry about dinner. I *did* remember to bring my plastic."

"I have cash. My mother always told me to have cab fare, so if my date got out of hand, I didn't have to rely on him for a ride home. Over the years I've found that to be excellent advice," Rachel said.

"I promise not to get out of hand," Blackie whispered just before the sari-clad hostess came to seat them.

The restaurant was small, with booths along one wall and a few tables in the middle. The walls were decorated with tapestries depicting scenes from Indian mythology and the epic tale, *The Mahabharata.* A faint scent of incense hung in the air and mingled pleasantly with the spices of the food.

The waiter lit the red candle on the table while they studied the menu.

"Are you familiar with Indian food?" Blackie asked.

"Yes. I like it because they fix great meatless dishes."

Blackie lowered his menu to look at Rachel. "Are you a vegetarian?"

"Whenever I can be one without raising a fuss." She felt his gaze on her. "Do you find that strange?"

"No. You're full of interesting surprises," he said. He reached for her hand. "No meat. No alcohol."

"I have a glass of wine occasionally, when it would create a scene or require a lengthy explanation if I didn't. It's the same with eating meat. When I have a choice, though, I'd rather not have either."

"One of these days I'm going to find out all about you. Your likes, your dislikes, your strengths, your weaknesses."

He already knew her weakness—a black-haired, blue-eyed alto sax player. Thank heaven he didn't realize it, Rachel reflected.

They ordered several dishes.

"You mentioned your mother. Where is she?" Blackie asked.

"She's remarried. Her husband is a career soldier, so they move around a lot."

"Is that why you chose to stay with your father when they divorced?"

"That was one reason. Another was that Evan listened to me when he was drinking when no one else could reach him."

"And you were, what? Fifteen? I think that's remarkable. You're remarkable."

"Hardly. I only did what I thought I had to do," Rachel said. "What about your family?

"I have an older brother, Ben. My parents are still married to each other."

"That's great. I've always thought how lucky children were who grew up in a normal, two-parent home," Rachel said, her voice soft and wistful.

"That doesn't guarantee happiness, you know."

Rachel saw the scowl on his handsome face and waited.

"Ben and I spent an awful lot of time with babysitters." Actually it was housekeepers and later boarding schools, but he couldn't reveal that without revealing that his family was wealthy.

"Did your mother have a career?"

"Not the kind you're thinking of." Blackie's low, sonorous voice had assumed a grim quality. "Her career consisted of playing bridge, beauty appointments, and dinner parties. She couldn't be bothered with two small boys."

Rachel heard the bitterness underneath the flippant tone he'd tried to assume. "And your father?"

"Too busy earning money so my mother could live the life she wanted and that he thought she ought to have."

So, Blackie's background was upper middle class. That surprised her. Judging by his present lifestyle, she had assumed he came from a working-class environment. Had he deliberately turned his back on his heritage? Odd, she mused. They'd almost exchanged lifestyles. She had rejected the Bohemian milieu of her father's world for the comforts of middle-class life, and Blackie had rejected that in favor of an artistic existence. Was the irony of this fate's subtle warning?

"A penny for your thoughts."

Rachel snapped out of her speculations. "I was just

thinking how much simpler it is to take care of pets. All they require is simple affection, food, and shelter. Children seem to need so much more."

"I don't know about that. If the affection is genuine and includes nurturing, the rest is pretty much the same. You meet the physical, mental, and emotional needs of your pets. Seems to me that's what you do for children too."

Their needs weren't met by one parent's leaving, she reflected.

"You look grim," Blackie observed.

Rachel's look brightened. "I didn't mean to. And it's not the company either."

The appetizers arrived and were as spicy as Rachel had hoped. She refilled both their water glasses. "So, what did you do before you started to create a sensation on the Chicago jazz scene a year ago?" she asked, and she watched his face closely. It was almost as if a veil had been lowered over his eyes.

"Oh, this and that. You know."

"No, I don't know." She looked at him expectantly.

"I studied the sax for many years while earning a living outside of music." He wasn't lying, exactly, he thought. Just skirting the truth a little.

"Formal studies? Or on your own?"

"Both. At first I studied with teachers and then on my own."

"Why did you wait so long before you started to perform in public?"

"I didn't think I was good enough."

No, he wasn't the kind of man who'd do anything

unless he could do it well. A perfectionist. She should have known that.

The waiter served the main courses. "Would you like to try some of my eggplant?" she offered.

"Yes, please." Blackie leaned forward and opened his mouth.

Rachel hadn't expected to feed him, and the intimate act flustered her a little, but she managed to place a forkful between those gleaming white teeth. The amused, warm glitter in his eyes told her that he was aware of her feelings.

"My turn," he announced. He held out his fork toward her. Not wanting to admit that this caused her pulse to flutter like sails in a gale, Rachel opened her mouth and took the food.

"Shades of *Tom Jones*," Blackie said, and he grinned engagingly. "I always thought he had the right idea."

"You would," Rachel murmured, but she didn't manage to sound disapproving. "Do you believe in reincarnation?"

He looked surprised. "I don't know. I haven't given it much thought. Why?"

"Because in one of your previous lives, you were definitely a rake. I have absolutely no doubt about that."

He chuckled.

"Come to think about it, I'm not sure you aren't one in this life."

His chuckle deepened. He shook his dark head. "Not in this life. I don't have the time to be dissolute."

"But you'd like to be?"

"Don't know. I might, if you were dissolute with me. How about it?"

"You've got the leer down," Rachel said, observing the gleam in his eyes and the inviting curve of his lips.

He laughed, spoiling the seductive expression. "I told you. You are good for me. You make me laugh and feel young again."

"As if you were old," she scoffed. With that aura of vitality he would never be old. As long as that fire burned in him, the fire that transformed every note he played into an unforgettable experience, he'd be young in heart and mind.

"Have you thought of a title for the album yet?"

"No." Actually, he'd been toying with titles like, "Silver Eyes," "Lady Love," "Gray-eyed Madonna," and other similar, sentimental, self-indulgent titles, none of which he could use. After all, he wasn't the only performer on the record.

"How much of the music on the record will be original?"

"About three-fourths."

Rachel was momentarily speechless. He'd said that modestly and unaffectedly, as if it were not in the least impressive.

"Evan contributed two numbers. They're both good, but one is outstanding. Wait till you hear it," Blackie said.

"I knew you were both talented, but I didn't realize just how talented you are," Rachel murmured.

"How did you know I was talented at composing?" he asked.

"Your 'apology,' remember? That witty little composition that was just a little tongue-in-cheek, a little teasing, a little . . ."

"Go on," he encouraged.

". . . seductive and a little naughty."

He grinned at her happily. "You understood. Good. And we have time to let our feelings grow. Like music. You can't hurry or force a great performance. It's got to flow naturally, or it isn't worth a plugged nickel."

Was Blackie assuring her that he'd give her time, or did his feelings for her stand on a threshold, either to develop into something worthwhile or to die a spontaneous death? Rachel didn't know which possibility she preferred or if she wanted either one. All she knew was that he'd thrown her heart and soul into chaos. The best thing, her brain insisted, was to get away from the source that had caused this perilous turmoil.

She glanced at her watch.

"What's the matter? Bored with me already?" he asked, a dangerous gleam in his bright eyes.

Bored? If only that were the case, Rachel thought. No man had ever bored her less or thrown her further off the calm, efficient course of her life.

"No, I'm not bored. I've really enjoyed our dinner, but I have to take food to Mrs. Moore, and she goes to bed at eleven. I'm sorry, but I'll have to call it a night."

Blackie signaled for the check. "Is Mrs. Moore a shut-in?"

"Oh, no. She's one of the people who volunteers to board animals for us when the shelter runs out of space."

"We're talking cat kibble and dog food?" Blackie asked.

"Don't look so put out. Have you ever been in a room with twelve cats all demanding to be fed at the same time?"

"Can't say that I have."

Rachel waited until he'd signed the charge slip before she spoke. "Believe me, you don't want to hear that racket, and you don't want to wish it on sweet, old Mrs. Moore either. Besides, it's not as if I'm leaving you for another man," she pointed out.

"That's true," he acknowledged, and his face cheered up. "Witchy-woman, it's hard to stay upset with you," he admitted. "I suppose I shouldn't have told you that. Tactical error on my part."

The bleak, wary look in his eyes a moment before had touched her. "I don't play games. Not unless you force me to," she assured him.

He studied her intently and at length. "Then you're a rare gem of a woman," he said, his voice and expression solemn.

Outside, the night was mild and starlit. "Let's walk," Rachel suggested impulsively. "It's only a few blocks, and the night is beautiful."

"And so are you." Blackie gazed into her startled eyes and, leaning down, brushed his lips over hers. Then he drew her arm through his. "Okay. We'll walk."

They strolled in silence for a while, his arm warm against hers, her full skirt swinging against his leg.

"Tell me about Mrs. Moore," he requested.

"There isn't much to tell. She's retired, a widow, her children are grown and have left home, and so she volunteered to take in cats whenever we don't have enough space for them. We investigated her, of course. We wouldn't entrust the care of our animals to just anyone. You have no idea what people are capable of. We need more people like her. Some days there just isn't room, and then the animals have to be . . . put to sleep. What a euphemism!"

Hearing the raw pain in her voice, Blackie put his arm around her shoulders. "You are doing something to help."

"But it's so little, and the problem is so immense," she said passionately. "We have to get statutes passed against all sorts of terrible practices that the law still allows. To lobby for that and to establish new shelters, we have to raise money. Big money."

"You will. You'll come up with a great fund-raising idea. As passionately as you feel about the animals, you'll think of something," Blackie assured her.

"I hope so." Rachel sighed and nestled closer against him.

When they arrived at her house, he pulled her inside the circle of his arms and held her protectively. "You have a soft, compassionate heart, Rachel Carradine. That makes you special and precious. I like a woman with a warm, caring nature." He kissed her gently, reverently, and time stood still.

Chapter Seven

"**I**ll? Evan is ill?" Fear and guilt in equal proportions encircled Rachel's heart and squeezed—fear because her father had never taken care of himself, and guilt because she'd been so involved with the new ad campaign that she hadn't taken time to stop by the club.

Work wasn't the only reason she hadn't been to The Blues in the Night, she admitted to herself with abject shame. She'd been reluctant to see Blackie again, reluctant because the evening they'd spent together had put a dent the size of the Grand Canyon into her defenses against him.

"Take it easy." Donna's voice flowed soothingly through the telephone receiver. "The doctor says it's a mild respiratory infection. Nothing to worry about."

"It's bad enough for you to have called in a doctor?" Rachel asked, her voice quavering with anxiety.

"Only because I know this physician well, and he owed me a few favors," Donna explained.

Rachel rubbed the back of her neck, trying to ease the sudden tension that had settled there. "I don't understand," she said.

"My ex-husband is a physician. I called him to look at Evan because I didn't like the sound of his cough."

"Is your ex-husband a *good* physician?"

"Yes. He was a lousy husband, but he's an excellent doctor."

"Oh." Rachel tried to assimilate this information as well as purge her usually logical, analytical mind of the paralyzing anxiety that still held it in its grip. "Did the doctor prescribe something for Evan?"

"Yes. A cough syrup, lots of liquids, and bed rest. I also put a mustard plaster on Evan's chest. You should have heard him complain about that."

"I can imagine. He always was a lousy patient." A mustard plaster, Rachel mused. She had great respect for old herbal remedies and folk medicine. "Do you think I should hire a private nurse?" Rachel inquired. "I can't take time off right now to nurse him, and it isn't fair for you to have to do it by yourself."

"I don't mind. Rachel, he really isn't seriously ill, though from the way he carries on, you'd think he was."

Donna's voice was affectionate, and Rachel smiled. Evan would play the invalid for all it was worth. "Tell Evan that I'll be by to see him before I fly to New Jersey. And thanks, Donna."

After she hung up, Rachel frowned. It had been

easy to promise to swing by Evan's apartment, but now that she looked at her appointment book, she realized she'd been overly optimistic. She'd have to cancel a few appointments and reschedule others, but it could be done. She dialed the security department's number.

"Dennis, do we have anyone who could run a couple of errands for me before I catch my plane?"

"Let me see," he said, checking his log. "The new kid, Bryan, but we don't have a company car available for him to drive."

"That's no problem. I have a car," Rachel volunteered.

"Okay. I'll send him right in."

A sober-faced, clean-cut young man entered her office only minutes later.

"I want you to pick up the flowers I ordered and a quart of chicken soup. The addresses of the florist and the deli are on this list. Bring me the receipts." Rachel handed the list and a couple of bills to Bryan. "Here are the keys to my car. It's the green Mustang in parking space number two."

Rachel chaired two meetings. Sticking scrupulously to the agenda of each and cutting off all superfluous digressions, she finished fifteen minutes early. That allowed her to spend a few minutes with her menagerie at home before she called a taxi. She asked the driver to wait in front of Evan's apartment.

Her father didn't look as bad as Rachel had feared. Donna had brought in extra pillows to prop him up comfortably. A humidifier misted the air, and a pitcher of lemonade sat on the nightstand. Soothing classical music floated softly from the stereo, and Rachel realized that Evan was receiving excellent care. She relaxed for the first time that day.

"Don't come any closer," Evan warned. "I don't want you to catch this bug. It's bad enough that Donna is going to come down with it, but she won't listen to reason and go home," Evan complained, but the look he sent the quiet blond woman didn't match his querulous voice.

"I told you I won't catch your virus. After teaching kindergarten all those years, I developed immunities to everything," Donna claimed.

A kindergarten teacher. An ex-husband who was a physician. This woman was obviously more complex than Rachel had considered or wanted her to be, she admitted to herself. Donna was worth getting to know, so Rachel resolved to invite her to lunch or dinner as soon as the pressure of her work eased.

"So. How are you feeling?" she asked her father.

"Better already," he assured her.

"One more mustard plaster and we'll have this thing licked," Donna promised.

"The only reason I'm letting you put this stuff on my chest is that I don't want my fans switching their allegiance to the new piano player Blackie hired to fill in for me."

"They wouldn't do that," Rachel soothed. "You know he can't possibly be anywhere near as brilliant as you are." Evan looked mollified. "I brought you chicken soup," Rachel said, and she set the heavy carton on the dresser. "The flowers were supposed to cheer you up, but I see that you've already got someone here to do that."

"They're nice," Evan said.

"Let me put these beauties into a vase," Donna offered.

Rachel handed her the striking bouquet of blue-and-yellow irises.

"Thanks, sugar. So you're off to the plant again? Blackie asked where you've been. I didn't know what to tell him."

"Evan, you know how busy I am when we get a new campaign going," she pointed out.

The keen blues eyes under the bushy brows regarded her levelly. "Is that the only reason you haven't been to the club?"

"What other reason could there be?" Rachel hoped she didn't sound as evasive as she felt.

"I can think of one. Tall, dark, brilliant. Deep enough to have feelings and passion for his music *and* the woman he cares about. Rachel, that's a combination you find once in a blue moon. Don't throw it away out of prejudice or pride."

"I seem to remember meeting someone like that before."

Evan snorted derisively. "Earl was a one-note man. Blackie's the whole register. You think about that."

Donna's return with the flowers mercifully ended a conversation that was throwing Rachel's thoughts and emotions into turmoil. She didn't want to think of Blackie at all, much less in such a favorable light.

"Think about what I said," Evan exhorted when she was ready to leave. He blew her a kiss. When Donna walked her to the door, he called after Rachel, "Remember to compare a jingle to a ballad, a pop tune to a concerto."

"I assume you know what Evan means by that?" Donna asked.

"Yes. Thanks for taking care of him." Impulsively Rachel hugged Donna. The older woman's face lit up with joy as she hugged Rachel back.

In the taxi, Rachel leaned back against the seat and closed her eyes. A ballad. A concerto. Evan was right. Blackie was all those and more. It wasn't fair to compare him to Earl or to anyone else. Blackie was unique. And, at least as a musician, he was exceptional.

As a man too, the emotional, womanly side of her insisted insidiously. Maybe, her rational mind conceded, but that was a problem she'd have to face later. Right now she had to make some decisions involving millions of dollars that could mean the difference between Athena, Inc., ending the year in the black or in the red.

With that sobering thought she sat up, took a folder from her briefcase, and forced her attention away from that beguiling, talented man and onto the stark, uncompromising figures on the pages before her.

Three days later Blackie waited for her at the airport. "Rachel? Rachel?"

Looking tired, she turned in the direction of the

sound, but she didn't appear to have the strength to break through the throng surrounding her.

He grabbed her, and, shielding her with his body, he extricated her from the crush of humanity. He pulled her into the doorway of a closed office.

"Are you okay?" he asked.

"Oh, sure." Rachel nodded her head languorously.

"We have to get your bag. You did take one to New Jersey with you, didn't you?"

"Bag? Oh, yes. I have a bag. Somewhere." She waved a hand vaguely.

"Rachel, honey, what's the matter?"

"Matter? Why, nothing. Everything's taken care of. We'll first produce five hundred thousand bottles of Amour," she recited. "Then we'll tear down the production line and set up for the ladies' astringent and then the men's toner and then . . ."

"Rachel, hush." Blackie placed a hand under her chin and raised her face. Her lovely features exuded total exhaustion. Not even the skillfully applied makeup could hide the pallor of her skin or the purplish blue shadows under her beautiful eyes. "When was the last time you slept?" he demanded.

She shook her head. "Can't sleep. Have to go to New Jersey and figure out the production schedule," she rambled. "Can't stop till it's all set up."

Blackie realized that she was too exhausted for rational dialogue. "That's right. I'll go with you," he murmured comfortingly. He placed an arm around her waist in support.

"That's sweet," she said, smiling wanly, "but you don't have to. I've made the trip so often, I could do it with my eyes closed. See?" she said, closing her eyes.

"No, honey. Don't close your eyes yet. Maybe later. Okay?" He needed her to stay awake until he got her into a cab. After that she could sleep and probably would. He'd carry her into her house and put her to bed. A great tenderness welled up inside him, and he pulled her closer against him.

They approached the luggage carousel. "What color is your bag?" Blackie asked. "Never mind." There was only one suitcase left circling, and he grabbed it. The name tag identified the beige leather bag as hers.

"Here we go. Just a few more steps," he encouraged. Imperiously he motioned to an approaching taxi, and it stopped. While the driver put the suitcase into the trunk, Blackie helped Rachel into the backseat.

Miraculously she regained some strength, and her earlier confusion disappeared. "How'd you know I'd be on this flight?"

"Evan told me. He was a little worried. Thought you sounded tired when he talked to you."

"Tired. Heavens, yes. We're all wiped out, but we got the job done. Blackie, do you have any idea how complicated it is to schedule production? I mean, you can't just do it arbitrarily. That would cost too much in time and money. Did you know that for some cosmetics, part of the previous production line can be used again?"

"No, I didn't." Talk about getting her second wind, he thought admiringly.

"Well, it can. So you have to look at what products you need and how to group the production of items for maximum efficiency. Sounds simple, doesn't it?"

"Not to me, it doesn't."

"Maybe not simple. It just takes a certain way of thinking. This may sound conceited. I don't mean it to be—"

"What does?" Blackie encouraged.

"I'm good at that kind of analysis and problem-solving. Of course, I'm absolutely no good at what you're brilliant at. Do you know I never even attempted to learn to read music? Isn't that pitiful?"

Blackie smiled. Exhaustion had the same effect on Rachel as several margaritas had on other people. He'd never heard her talk so uninhibitedly, and he found it innocently charming. "Reading music isn't so hard. With your logical mind, I could teach you in no time."

"You could? Will you, Blackie?"

When she looked at him with those enormous, mauve-lidded gray eyes, he'd give her anything she asked for. "Of course I will."

"Good. I was so aggravated when you had the sheet music delivered to me and I had no idea what it would sound like."

"So, you wondered," Blackie murmured with immense satisfaction. Briefly he questioned why Evan had never attempted to teach her, but perhaps he had, and Rachel had refused. Now was definitely not the time to go into the father-daughter relationship between these two remarkable people he was so drawn to. He leaned over and gently kissed her hair.

"Here we are," he announced some time later. "Come." Rachel took his hand obediently and let him help her out of the cab.

The taxi had already pulled away when Rachel fumbled through her handbag. "I owe you for the fare," she mumbled, thrusting a bill at him.

Knowing this was no time to argue over money with her, he took it. "Want me to help you look for your key?" he asked.

Wordlessly she handed him her handbag. He rummaged through it for the key and unlocked the door. As he dropped the key back into her purse, he also slid the bill back into a side compartment.

He watched Rachel rush forward to hug the dog who hurled himself at her. Then she approached the three cats, who waited with patient dignity to receive their share of affection.

"Lucky creatures," he murmured not without a trace of envy. "I'll take your bag to your bedroom. Upstairs?" he asked, inclining his head toward the stairs.

"Mmm. First door at the top." Rachel was sitting on the floor, heedless of the expensive suit she was wearing, receiving wet dog kisses and stroking the purring cats.

Blackie entered her bedroom but stopped in surprise when he saw the bed. *Glory be,* he thought, and he grinned delightedly. His eyes took in the rest of the room: the simple, elegant lines of the furniture, the delicate blue-and-white wallpaper, the gleaming wood floor with the Aubusson rug. Yes, all that matched Rachel's sophisticated appearance, but her bed was as much at odds with the rest of the room as her lush mouth was with the classic lines of her face.

He didn't know enough about antique furniture to pinpoint the bed's style, but it was definitely endowed with the seductive charm of an earlier era. Soft, sheer white curtains hung from the four tall corner posts of the bed. Shorter flounces draped the canopy above it. Tentatively he pulled at the curtains, catching his breath when he realized that the bed could be completely enclosed with the cloud-soft fabric.

He wiped the damp palm of his free hand on his jeans, then forced himself to turn his back on the enticing bed.

He looked around the room, undecided about where to put the suitcase. At home he dumped his bag onto his bed, but he didn't think Rachel would appreciate his doing that to her delicate spread. A wicker chest in the corner looked sturdy enough.

When he opened the suitcase to remove her toiletries and her gown and robe, he felt a little like a voyeur. But Rachel was totally exhausted, he reasoned, and he was only trying to help.

"Rachel, are you all right?" He found her curled up on the hall rug with her pets ranged around her like sentries. "Honey, you can't sleep on the floor," he protested.

"S'comfortable," she murmured, trying desperately to get her eyes to open.

"No, no. Up you go." Blackie gently pulled her up. She was almost as limp as a rag doll as she leaned into him. He scooped her into his arms and carried her upstairs. She snuggled against him. As he felt the warmth of her breath on his neck, a delicious shiver tickled along his spine.

"Honey, I'm going to have to put you down so you can change out of your suit. Your nightgown is on the bed," he said. He set her on her feet and folded back the bedspread.

"I'll wait outside. Call me when you're in bed so I can say good night."

A few minutes later she called his name. He went to her and with gentle fingers moved the fine, dark hair that had fallen over her face. She seemed to be asleep already. He couldn't resist kissing one silken cheek. "Sleep well, Rachel." He turned off the light and quietly closed the door.

The sensation was pleasant, toe-curlingly pleasant, and Rachel instinctively moved her face toward the source of the sensuous delight.

"Wake up, honey."

Blackie's sexy voice. She'd never before heard a voice so clearly in a dream. Suddenly she was wide awake. Her eyes flew open. The source of the intense pleasure, she discovered, was Blackie's silken beard brushing against her cheek.

Sensing her alertness, he lifted his head and grinned. "I was beginning to think you'd never wake up."

"How long have I been asleep?" she murmured, disoriented.

Blackie glanced at his watch. "About fourteen hours."

"Good heavens. I've got to get up."

Blackie gently pushed her back onto the pillow. "Take it easy. I called Athena and told them you got in exhausted and couldn't come to work until after you'd rested. I have a mind to speak to your beloved Laura. Doesn't she know we abolished slavery over a century ago? Where does that woman get off, making you work so hard?" Blackie demanded, his black eyebrows pulled into a ferocious frown.

"Laura didn't make me work that hard. I did."

"Why?"

Rachel thought for a moment about her answer. What it came down to was that she hadn't wanted to spend any more time at the plant, so they'd put in overtime and finished the planning early. She had wanted to come home because she missed . . . No, she wasn't ready to admit that to herself, much less to the man bent over her, his appealing face only inches from hers.

Rachel became acutely aware of his body heat, of the scent of the soap he'd used. French-milled, the professional in her told her, and infinitely appealing, the woman in her acknowledged. What was he doing, sitting on her bed, one muscular forearm resting on the pillow beside her head? How long . . . What . . . ?

Blackie saw the realization of her predicament dawn on her lovely face, and he fought down an amused grin.

"I don't remember last night very clearly," Rachel began hesitantly. "For instance, what are you doing here this morning?" she asked, hoping her voice sounded more in control than she felt.

"First, it's noon, not morning. Second, I came back after our last set at the club and spent the night here." He watched her thick lashes fly up in confusion. She looked at him in alarm for an instant before the panic subsided. Most of it, anyway.

"I know nothing happened," she stated forcefully and with conviction. At least she hoped she sounded that certain.

"What makes you so sure?" Blackie challenged softly, a dangerous gleam in his blue eyes. "After all, here I am, and you do remember my carrying you upstairs, turning the bed down . . ." Deliberately he left the sentence hanging there. He watched warm pink color tinge her fair skin and perceived the momentary flicker of doubt in the gray depths of her eyes.

Confusion muddled Rachel's mind for a second. Yes, she remembered all that and then . . . nothing. She looked deeply into his bright, hypnotic eyes. "I'm certain nothing happened last night," she claimed at last, challenging him to deny it.

He grinned. "True. You were way too tired for anything but sleep."

He lowered his face and kissed the hollow at the base of her throat. For a moment she abandoned herself to the sweet sensation and stroked his beautiful dark, dark hair. Realizing what she was doing, she went rigid with shock.

Feeling her reaction, Blackie raised his face to look searchingly at her.

She took advantage of the respite to pull the sheet up to her chin like a suit of armor. "You still haven't told me why you came last night," she stammered, her eyes lowered.

He straightened up, giving her space to compose herself. "The truth?"

"Yes, please. I always prefer it."

"Because I was worried about you."

"Why?" she asked, truly puzzled.

"Because you were so exhausted, I was afraid you'd sleep through a dozen smoke alarms going off at the same time if a fire should start in the house."

"Oh."

"And because I wanted to be near you."

"Oh." Great. She sounded like a monosyllabic moron, Rachel thought. "Where did you sleep?" she couldn't help asking.

"Would you believe me if I told you I slept next to you?"

She wavered only for a moment. "No." She'd have sensed his presence even in sleep.

"I looked in on you at three this morning, and you hadn't stirred, so how can you be so convinced that I didn't slip in beside you?"

"Analytical deduction. That side of the bed hasn't

been slept on," she pointed out triumphantly. She smiled saucily at him.

"I think I liked it better when you were dead tired and half asleep. You were more malleable then."

"Too bad," she retorted without sympathy. "Personally I think malleable is boring unless you're a metalworker."

He chuckled. "While you shower or bathe, I'll fix some food. What do vegetarians eat for breakfast?"

"As hungry as I am now, anything that doesn't move."

"Okay." He smiled and touched her sleep-tangled hair softly before he left her.

Chapter Eight

"Hello, Trio. Come here, puss. Don't you remember me? I won't hurt you," Rachel crooned softly. The three-legged cat hobbled toward her outstretched hand, and Rachel noted joyously that he'd made considerable progress. His gait was much less awkward. She rubbed his whiskers and scratched him behind his ears until he purred loudly, his green eyes half-closed in pure bliss.

"That one doesn't quite trust me yet," Blackie said, standing in the kitchen doorway.

"Considering that it was probably an adult man who hurt him, it'll be a while before he trusts males again," Rachel explained.

"I'm amazed that he learned to trust you so quickly."

Rachel smiled. "I think I was a cat in my last incarnation. That would explain the natural affinity."

With the innate grace of her sleek body, Blackie had no trouble believing that. She wore a light gray suit with a slightly deeper gray blouse, emphasizing her striking eyes. The monochromatic look was modified by a bright batik silk scarf fastened ascot style around her neck.

"You look none the worse for wear," he said. "As a matter of fact, you look beautiful." He reached for her, his hands urging but not forcing her. When she came willingly into his arms and kissed his mouth, his last coherent thought was that the day couldn't get any better than that.

Rachel kept her arms around his neck when she ended the kiss. She pulled back to look at him, and, striving for a light, cheerful tone despite her rapid heartbeat, she asked, "What did you fix for breakfast?"

"A rare treat," he promised. "Oatmeal."

Knowing there was no instant oatmeal in her kitchen, Rachel expected a gray, lumpy mess. Silently she vowed that even if it tasted like scorched, wet cement, she'd eat it all and thank Blackie for his effort. "I love oatmeal."

"Good. I let Piccolo out into the backyard. Is that okay?"

"Sure. He gets his morning exercise running along the fence that parallels the alley. I swear he smirks when he beats a car to the end of the yard."

Blackie laid an arm around her shoulders and led her to the kitchen. He pulled out a chair for her. "Madam?"

"Thank you."

Blackie had set two places at the table. He poured freshly brewed coffee and two glasses of orange juice and served each of them a bowl of oatmeal.

Encouraged by its smooth appearance, Rachel tasted it. "Why, this is perfect. Do you usually fix oatmeal for yourself?"

"Nope. This was my first time."

She stared at him speechlessly.

"I just followed the directions on the tin," he explained, pleased by the approving expression on Rachel's face.

"Then you're a natural cook," Rachel stated. "People usually judge cooking ability by fancy dishes, but I think you can discover natural talent by how the simple things turn out. You know, like oatmeal, or mashed potatoes and gravy."

He smiled happily.

"I know taking time out for me has to interfere with your plans for the day. I thought Evan said you'd be back in the studio today."

"Tomorrow. I wanted Evan to have another day of rest."

"Isn't that going to cost you a fortune?" Rachel asked worriedly. "I might be able to help out with the studio fee for today," she offered.

"Thanks, but that's not necessary. The studio wasn't booked per day."

"Oh. Are the facilities first-rate?" She didn't want Evan's first chance at releasing a record in years to come off shabbily.

"Uh-huh. It just changed hands, and the new owner renamed it Allegro. Do you like the name?"

"Yes, very much. It has a classy ring to it."

And he liked her. She certainly was a classy lady, but

he had a feeling he ought not to tell her that quite yet. Instead he refilled her coffee cup. "In the taxi last night you talked about how complicated it was to schedule production of cosmetics. Surely you're not the only one responsible for that, are you?"

Oh, dear, Rachel thought, alarmed. What else had she told him last night? She couldn't remember. It was all one hazy blur. "Oh, lots of people are involved in it. There's a production manager, a production engineer, a plant foreman, a foreman for each line, and so on," she explained. What she didn't say was that ultimately she *was* responsible. If something went wrong, the proverbial buck stopped at her desk.

She glanced at her watch. "This is nice, and I hate to be so rude and eat and run, but I have to go," she said, genuine regret on her face. She carried her dishes to the sink, rinsed them, and stacked them in the dishwasher. Blackie did the same with his.

"Can I give you a lift somewhere?" she offered.

His Porsche was parked down the street. "No. I'll walk. I need to stretch my legs."

And nice legs they were, Rachel thought—long, lean and muscular in well-worn jeans. "Thanks for breakfast and for last night—picking me up and everything."

"No thanks are necessary," Blackie said, "but I need another kiss, if you can spare one."

It would be quite safe to kiss him, Rachel decided. After all, they were two adults standing in a sunlit kitchen. Besides, there hadn't exactly been a run on her

kisses lately, she thought wryly. "I might be able to spare one," she told him, her voice studiedly casual.

"I was hoping you'd say that." With the slightly rough pad of one thumb he traced the full, sexy shape of her mouth. Though she'd put on makeup, she'd left her lips natural. She probably hadn't intended it to be an invitation to be kissed, Blackie thought, but that's how he perceived it.

Rachel had expected a quick, light kiss, followed by her hasty exit out the door, but Blackie appeared to have far different plans for her. He seemed to be fascinated with touching her mouth and looking at it as if they had all the time in the world. Perhaps he was content with that, but the longer he spent doing only that, the less content Rachel grew. It took considerable willpower on her part not to shift her weight from one foot to the other, to fidget, or simply to rise on tiptoe and kiss him senseless.

"You have the most fascinatingly shaped mouth," Blackie murmured at last. He tore his gaze away from it to study her face. "Your eyebrows—the way they're almost a straight line—give your face character and keep it from being perfect."

"Thanks. Statements like that are guaranteed to make my day," Rachel said.

"You misunderstand. I'd admire your face if it were perfect, but I wouldn't find it half as fascinating. Your face will never be boring, and I'll never get tired of looking at it." He saw her eyes light up with pleasure at his simple, sincere words. "Isn't that much better than perfect?" He cradled her face between his hands and kissed her softly. "Isn't it?" he asked again.

"If you say so." Rachel couldn't remember the question, but when his persuasive mouth touched hers, she felt like agreeing with whatever he claimed. When they broke apart, he blinked as if he, like she, was surprised to find himself still in a place as mundane as her kitchen.

After the initial shock Rachel thought, thank heaven for the mundane and prosaic. It pulled her back to reality and the necessity for caution. "I have to go," she murmured, and she moved away from Blackie. "I'm awfully late as it is," she added apologetically.

She picked up her briefcase from the hall table and fled outside to the safety of her car. Her fingers trembled as she inserted the key in the ignition.

Blackie watched her drive off. In some ways Rachel was smarter than he. She hadn't initiated this thing between them, and she was fighting it. That's what he should be doing. He hadn't thought so before, but now he was beginning to think that course of action wise. He was involved in producing what arguably could be an extraordinary recording, and nothing and no one ought to distract him from that. How often in a lifetime did a man have a chance to create something that would live on long after he was dead?

He had expected the sessions to go well after they'd played together for weeks at The Blues in the Night. What he hadn't expected was that musicians would be able to produce his music the way he'd heard it in his head. That didn't happen very often. Often? Whom was he kidding? Not even he could reproduce those perfect notes he heard in his mind every time. He should be concentrating solely on the music. His music.

He had turned his business matters over to his brother and his assistants for the duration of the recording sessions, but he wasn't fool enough to turn Rachel over to anyone. She haunted him.

Rachel. He should banish her from his life and purge her from his thoughts. *Fat chance,* he thought derisively. Before she'd set foot back into town, he'd rushed off to meet her at the airport. He even thought of her off and on when he played. That was a first. Always before he could dismiss everything and everyone from his mind but the music.

"Citywide we have to raise a quarter of a million dollars if we are to maintain the animal shelters we now have, plus set up three more," Rachel announced, her gaze sweeping over the members of the board sitting around the table in the community room of the oldest branch of the public library.

"Do we have to have *three* new animal shelters?" the treasurer of the Chicago chapter of the Animal Lovers Society asked.

In some ways Seth reminded Rachel of Henry, but where Henry was built along the lines of a lean, nervy greyhound, Seth looked more like a chubby, satisfied dachshund.

"Yes, we need three," Rachel said, her voice firm. "Most of our foster caretakers are elderly people who frequently need emergency medical attention. Then we have to scramble to find places for their boarders. Three new shelters should alleviate the overcrowding in our existing shelters and allow for temporary placement of our family-boarded animals."

"Let's vote," Felicia Foreman said.

Rachel suppressed a smile. Felicia was always ready to get on with things. Attractive, well-put-together, she was the perfect young matron, mainstay of the Junior League, the PTA, and other organizations lucky enough to have garnered her enthusiastic support. Patience, however, wasn't her strong suit.

The vote was unanimous. Now they had to figure out how to raise the money.

"How about an auction?" Felicia suggested. "You know, everybody donates an item, some white elephant, an antique they hate or have grown tired of, or something from their business. We can invite all our friends who can spare a hundred dollars or so, provide some domestic champagne, soft drinks, and canapés, and we're in business."

"Do you actually raise any money with that approach?" Seth asked, his entire body revealing his skepticism.

Felicia waved a slender, burgundy-nailed hand in his direction. "Oh, sure. We do it all the time."

"Since she's the expert on auctions, I nominate Felicia as the chairperson. Do I hear a second?" Rachel asked.

Seth seconded the motion, and the motion passed. With her expertise and connections, Felicia was perfect for the task.

"We will, of course, all help," Rachel pointedly reminded the members before they adjourned.

"Where are these auctions usually held?" Rachel asked as she walked out with Felicia.

"All depends what they're for. Sometimes in fancy tents set up on the spacious lawns of country estates. Sometimes in a public park or in the hall of the local Elks or VFW."

"With homeless animals as the cause, where do we rank?" Rachel asked, her curiosity aroused.

"Hmm. Somewhere below the symphony yet above the preservation of cobblestone streets," Felicia replied without hesitation.

Rachel thought at first that this was a joke, but then she remembered that Felicia's sense of humor was severely limited.

They parted in the parking lot. For a few seconds Rachel debated with herself before turning her car in the direction of the club. She really shouldn't be seeing Blackie again so soon. At least not after the breakfast they'd shared.

The traffic light changed to yellow, and Rachel stopped. She could make a right-hand turn here and drive home. She hesitated, but when the light turned green, she stepped on the gas pedal and shot straight through the intersection. "You're playing with fire," she muttered to herself uselessly, knowing that she would proceed to The Blues in the Night no matter what.

The moment she entered the club, her spirits soared. Evan was pounding the keys with relentless energy. Rachel didn't know the name of the number, but she recognized the riveting eight-beats-to-the-bar-and-repeated-bass-riff style of the boogie-woogie. There wasn't a foot in the club that wasn't tapping out the rhythm or a body not swaying to its throbbing beat. When Blackie's sax jumped in, repeating the howling, raw, earthy, ancient demands of the blood, the set built to a shattering crescendo.

Rachel picked up the wine list from the table and fanned herself. It didn't surprise her that the sextet took a break after that sizzling number. They had to be exhausted. How Blackie had spotted her so quickly, she didn't know, but she watched him pick his way purposefully toward her. Members of the audience interrupted his progress. He spoke briefly and smilingly to them but steadily drew nearer. The closer he came, the more vigorously Rachel fanned herself.

He pulled a chair close to hers and sat down. He raised an arm and used the rolled-up sleeve of his blue-and-white striped shirt to wipe his forehead. "The air-conditioning isn't working properly," he explained.

"Then why did you play that raw, emotional boogie number?" Rachel asked. "You must know what it does to the audience."

He reached for her hand and enfolded it in his. "What did the boogie do to you?"

As if that smiling, black-bearded charmer didn't know!

"Don't look away," he ordered softly.

Rachel's glance flew back to his in spite of herself. She felt like some small, furry creature held captive by his predatory gaze.

"What did the music make you feel?" he repeated in the same soft, melodic voice.

She shook her head in denial.

"Don't be a coward. Tell me."

"Not if I live to be a hundred."

His eyebrows rose, and the gleam in his eyes grew hotter. "You've told me what I wanted to know." He raised her hand to his mouth and gently kissed it.

Rachel's heart beat like a set of bongo drums, and her lungs felt as if they would explode. "Don't," she rasped, her mouth dry.

"Why?" he drawled lazily. "I know you're not scandalized or offended. It's a little late to pretend to be either."

"You're impossible. Insufferable, arrogant, conceited. I don't know why I even bother talking to you." For some reason she felt incredibly angry with him. She wanted to lash out at him. She tugged forcefully and finally succeeded in freeing her hand from his. Her scolding didn't seem to bother him.

"You're still fighting me," he said, as if he'd commented on the weather. "Deep down you know it's useless to fight this thing between us, don't you?"

It was only a rhetorical question, Rachel judged from his tone. She opened her mouth to deny his claim hotly, but in a blindingly honest instant she knew he was right. She clamped her lips together with grim determination. If she couldn't deny his claim, she'd be double blasted if she'd admit it.

"Rachel, Rachel," he chided softly. "No matter how hard you try to tighten that gorgeous mouth into the thin ridge of a harridan's disapproval, you won't succeed. Nature is against you. Thank heaven for that."

"Maybe I can't transform myself into a thin-lipped harridan, but how about a loud, aggressive, crockery-throwing one?" she challenged.

"We'll budget a certain amount of money each month for new plates."

He had the audacity to grin at her. Rachel made a grab for the glass ashtray on the table, but he was too quick for her. His hand clamped over hers.

"As much as I'd love to put that theory into practice, this isn't the right place. We have an audience," he said placidly.

"I'm so glad you made it tonight, sugar." Evan's hand landed on her shoulder from behind. "You remember Donna, don't you?"

"Of course. How are you?" Rachel asked the blond woman with a genuinely friendly smile. "Please join us. You survived Evan's convalescence okay?"

"Now, Rachel. I was a perfect lamb," her father insisted.

"Of course you were," Donna agreed with a wink at Rachel.

"How did your meeting go tonight?" Evan asked.

"We voted to create three new animal shelters. That was easy. The hard part will be coming up with the money."

"Any ideas?" Blackie asked.

"One of our board members suggested we hold an auction. So if you have any white elephants you want to get rid of, here's your chance."

"That's an excellent way to raise money," Blackie agreed. "Very little overhead." When he saw Rachel's astonished eyes, he knew he had to improvise something quickly. He wasn't ready to tell her that Blackstone J. Madigan was a perennial guest at fund-raising auctions. "A friend of mine held one to aid the musicians' fund."

"I kept this birdbath someone gave me eons ago. Don't ask me why," Donna said, "but it's sort of neat. The basin is like a huge, open rose."

"I have a huge ashtray in the shape of a baby grand piano," Evan offered.

"What are you featuring in the form of entertainment?" Blackie asked.

"Entertainment? I hadn't thought that was necessary."

"It's indispensable. Now, I happen to know of several jazz musicians who'd gladly donate their time," Blackie said.

"Great idea," Evan chimed in. "While the guests look at the offerings, we can provide background music."

"I'd love it, but you know we couldn't pay you," Rachel pointed out.

"I know. It's a donation. I'm sure Jawbone would

join us, and we can always get one of the young guys to sit in on the drums," Evan said. "It may not be the full sextet—"

"It doesn't have to be," Rachel interrupted. "A trio or a quartet would be fine. With you guys playing, we could get as many music lovers to attend as we do animal lovers." She smiled at her father and then turned back to Blackie.

The warmth of her smile sent the temperature of Blackie's blood soaring. Under the table he slipped out of one loafer and hooked his foot around Rachel's ankle. He felt her stiffen, but when she didn't move her foot, he stroked her ankle with his toes.

Even his foot was sexy, Rachel thought, dismayed. How could she resist a man whose every touch and gesture sent her pulse racing? It was a damned conspiracy, that's what it was. She didn't know what she'd done to get Cupid riled at her, but in one of his capricious moods he'd evidently decided to teach her a lesson. *Resist me, will you?* he seemed to taunt her. *Try it and see what happens. You'll fall in love, lady, deeply, hopelessly.* In her mind Rachel could hear the winged cherub's mischievous laughter.

"What do you say, Rachel?"

Startled, Rachel looked at her father with no idea what he'd been talking about.

"About the four of us going out to dinner Sunday night," he prompted.

"Oh?" Her mind feverishly weighed the pros and cons. It might be better if they came to her house. That way they would all come in one car and leave together, so temptation would be averted one more time.

"Why don't you come to my house for dinner? You won't even have to eat grains and berries," she joked. "I'll break down and fix my famous seafood casserole," she offered with a bright smile.

"I can vouch for that casserole," Evan said. "It's delicious."

"I'll throw in chocolate mousse for dessert," she tempted.

"Oh, that does it for me. I never could resist chocolate mousse," Donna declared.

"Sounds good," Blackie said, his voice oddly quiet.

Rachel looked at him, trying to guess what had brought shadows to his beautiful eyes. Evan and Donna excused themselves, going to another table to visit with friends.

They sat in strained silence, and Rachel hated it. Arguing with Blackie was better than this silence. Anything was. "My seafood casserole really isn't that bad," she began tentatively. "You can always fill up on potatoes and vegetables." Still no reaction.

"Why didn't you accept my invitation to dinner?" he asked. "It was my idea for the four of us to go out. What's the matter? Do you think I'd invite you if I couldn't afford to pay for dinner?"

So that's what this was all about, Rachel thought, relieved. During her imaginary confrontation with Cupid, she'd missed hearing Blackie's invitation. She'd have to mollify him without revealing her lapse of attention.

"No. But I wanted to make sure that we wouldn't end up someplace where Evan would be pressured into having a drink and I'd be served a slab of half-raw meat. So you see, my reasons were terribly selfish. I'm sorry. I didn't mean to hurt your feelings. Truly."

That was true. She didn't want to hurt Blackie. Ever. She slipped out of one pump and rubbed her toes against his ankle. She felt his body jerk as if a live current had passed through it.

This was fun, she discovered. Blackie hadn't slipped his loafer back on, so she took advantage of that. Her toes moved lower against his instep and then across his sole.

"You're ticklish," she murmured, delighted by the discovery. Smiling, she watched him bite his lip to keep from laughing. "Oh, Madigan, I've got you in my power now."

"Isn't that the truth, witchy-woman."

Chapter Nine

In her office Rachel picked up the intercom, her mind still busy with the progress report from the plant. Peggy was saying something about someone's wanting to see her. "I'm sorry, Peggy. Who's here?"

"A Blackie Madigan is downstairs."

"What?" Rachel shouted. She was almost immediately contrite. "Sorry, I didn't mean to yell."

"Who is this man? Shall I activate the silent alarm?" Peggy asked.

"No! Don't do that." Rachel looked around, panic-stricken for a moment before she realized there was no place she could hide. She'd known this moment would come sooner or later, but she had hoped for later. She took a deep breath. "Peggy, ask the security guard to send Mr. Madigan up."

As soon as she hung up, Rachel grabbed her compact from her purse and checked her face. She ran a brush through her hair and touched up her lip gloss. Then she took a bottle of Amour, sprayed it into the air six inches in front of her, and stepped into the descending cloud of fragrance. It was her favorite way of applying perfume.

She sat down behind her desk, folded her hands, but immediately jumped up. No, that was wrong. Too businesslike. She ran to the upholstered chairs grouped around a low, glass-topped table, but that seemed too informal. When she heard the bell announcing the arrival of the elevator, she rushed toward the open door of her office and stopped, undecided what to do. The sound of Blackie's voice immobilized her.

"Omigod. You're the man with the sexy voice," Peggy squealed.

Peggy, who'd parried the various and sundry passes of male buyers and salesmen with aplomb for years, had squealed like a teenager at Blackie Madigan.

Blackie stopped in Rachel's doorway, read the title embossed on the door, looked at her, and glanced at the lettering again. "Vice President of Production and Sales?"

Rachel flicked her tongue over her dry lips.

"You led me to believe that you demonstrated cosmetics in department stores," he said, his tone accusing. "That you did PR."

"No, I didn't. That's what you assumed my job was. Of course, I have demonstrated the use of our products in the past, and I will probably do so again in the future." If only she had some clue to his feelings. For once his expressive face was carefully guarded. "So, you see, it wasn't a lie exactly."

"But not exactly the truth either."

"No."

"Why, Rachel? Why didn't you tell me that you're a hotshot executive with a major corporation?" he demanded.

How could she explain without insulting him and hurting his feelings even more?

"Why?" he repeated, his face bleak.

"All right. I didn't correct your mistaken impression because men often react strangely to my title."

"Strangely?"

"Yes. In different ways, but generally oddly. With suspicion. If I were a male friend, and they discovered I was a vice president, they'd be impressed, glad for me, and ask about business."

"But since you're a woman?" he prompted.

Rachel shrugged. "They assume I slept my way to the top or clawed my way up, stepping over bodies."

Blackie listened to Rachel, completely surprised. He had never really considered a woman executive's position.

"Those who still want to date me usually want something from me. A job for a sister or for themselves, inside tips, free cosmetics, and so on. Now can you see why I wasn't too eager to reveal my position at Athena?"

"Yes." He understood completely. In his corporate persona he experienced the male version of the syndrome.

"I'm surprised Evan didn't let slip what your position is."

"Evan knows nothing about the cosmetics business. He thinks I have a well-paying office job of some sort and that the medical insurance policy I took out on him covers his periodic stays in rehab clinics."

"Which, of course, it doesn't," Blackie guessed.

"Not by a long shot."

"Well, I sort of suspected that you weren't exactly a lowly office employee when you returned from New Jersey," he admitted.

The smile he lavished on her was like a shaft of sunlight through thunderclouds. She blinked, surprised.

He caught her face between his hands and looked at her tenderly. "Rachel, I don't want or need a job for myself or my relatives. They're all employed and doing well. I've never asked a woman for money or other material things, and you'd be the last one I'd start that with. I would sooner die than live off you. Do you believe that?"

"Yes," she answered instantly and truthfully.

He bent and kissed her sweetly, caringly.

Rachel trembled. Though Blackie had kissed her more passionately in the past, there was something extra in this kiss, something new, something she couldn't define.

"The only thing I've ever been interested in is you," he murmured. "And you've known that from the moment we met. I never hid that, did I?"

"No." He hadn't. Heaven help her, from the instant

he'd asked her to go outside with him that first time, she'd known, and, heaven help her again, she had continued to see him. Rachel had walked open-eyed into this relationship, knowing he was a jazzman and despite all the negative vibrations that fact set off in her mind.

Blackie sensed her ambiguity and backed off. "Actually, I came here with a message. You're definitely going to have a quartet for your auction. Maybe even a quintet," he said.

"That's marvelous." Rachel threw her arms around his neck and hugged him hard. "I'll inform our publicity chairman. I bet we'll double the crowd because of you." Realizing she'd hugged him with the door open and everyone able to see, she backed off hastily.

"Would you like a tour of Athena?" she asked him.

"Is that the best offer I'm going to get?"

"My best and only offer. Take it or leave it."

"I'll take it."

Blackie followed her, met people, and listened attentively, but every time Rachel met his eyes, an anticipatory awareness passed between them like a tangible force.

"Too bad Laura isn't here. I'd have loved for you to meet her. She'll be at the auction, though," Rachel added.

They faced each other in the lobby of the executive floor, aware that people around them were eyeing them curiously.

"Will you be coming to the club before Sunday?" Blackie asked.

"I don't think so. Oh, not because I don't want to," she

assured him, "but tonight I won't leave here till late, and tomorrow I have to go to the grocery store, straighten up my house, and get ready for our Sunday dinner."

"Do you want me to bring anything?"

"No. Just yourself."

"I can do that," Blackie said, and he grinned. He lingered for a moment but couldn't put off leaving any longer. Horace had been circling the block for the past hour or so.

"Then we'll see each other Sunday evening."

Friday proved to be an exceedingly busy day, so when Peggy announced a call from Donna Williams, it took Rachel a second to realize that this was Evan's Donna.

"Rachel, I'm sorry to bother you at work, but I'd like for us to meet and talk."

"Is something wrong? Has Evan started to drink again?"

"No. Nothing like that, but it does concern Evan."

Enormously relieved, Rachel consulted her watch. "I can't leave here yet for three or four hours."

"That's okay. We could meet at the club. I'll be there all evening. Come when it's convenient," Donna suggested.

Rachel said she would, sensing that something important was up. She worked straight through, ignoring her protesting stomach, until her in-box was empty.

She arrived at the club in time to hear Evan announce that the Gregory Sextet would occasionally feature a vocalist. He introduced Donna, who looked every inch the part of a blues singer in a black, glittering, sequined dress that clung to her small waist and flowed smoothly over her rounded hips. Donna's rendition of "Lover-man, Where Can You Be?" was surprisingly professional. Rachel applauded vigorously.

After taking her bows, Donna came to Rachel's table.

"Let's go into the vestibule to talk," the blond suggested.

The sextet launched into a number Rachel didn't know but suspected was one of Blackie's compositions. She laid a hand on Donna's arm to detain her until the number ended.

"Wow. That was sensational," Rachel murmured, every cell in her body rocking with the primitive, hollering beat of the revival-camp-meeting-inspired number.

"One of Blackie's compositions," Donna confirmed, leading the way to the relatively quiet vestibule.

Donna seemed nervous, Rachel discovered, surprised. She hadn't appeared nervous singing before an audience, but now, face-to-face with her, she was.

"You looked and sounded good up there," Rachel said, hoping the compliment would put Donna at ease.

"Thank you, but that's not what I wanted to talk about."

"Okay, whatever it is, why don't you just say it?" Rachel encouraged.

Donna nodded, fingering the long string of pearls she wore. "Evan asked me to move in with him," she blurted out in a rush.

The announcement rendered Rachel temporarily speechless. In his many liaisons with women over the years Evan had never asked any of them to move in with him. This was serious. "I see. Have you decided to take him up on his offer?"

"I told him I'd have to talk to you first." Donna watched Rachel's eyes open wide in astonishment.

"Me? Why? I haven't lived with my father since before I married Earl years ago."

"I know that, but you're close. I respect that kind of affection and bond doubly because I was never lucky enough to have it," Donna said, her voice quiet, almost sad.

"Until now, I believe," Rachel corrected with a smile. She saw Donna's face light up.

"Do you really think so?" she questioned almost shyly.

"Yes." Rachel saw the tension ooze out of Donna's body, saw her nervous fingers release the string of pearls before it snapped. "I have absolutely no objections. Actually, I think Evan needs you. I realized that when I saw you nurse him. After all these years I think he's finally ready to settle down with one woman—you. If you'll have him. You know he's had problems—"

"I know," Donna interrupted. "He told me. I'm not some foolish young thing rushing idealistically into a relationship. I love Evan, but I'm not wearing blinders."

Rachel smiled broadly. "Then say yes to the man."

"I will."

The women hugged.

"I wouldn't mind getting one of those," Blackie's voice announced.

Donna turned, smiled with tears in her eyes, and said, "She's all yours," before she rushed back into the club.

"Don't I wish," Blackie murmured, sweeping Rachel into a firm hug. "You told me you couldn't come tonight. Not that I'm complaining," he assured her. He pressed a kiss against her fragrant, dark hair.

"Donna called, saying she had to see me."

"Oh?" Blackie released his hold on Rachel just enough to look into her face. "Problems?"

"I don't think so, but someone as undomesticated as you might consider it a disaster."

"That does it. I'm taking you home with me tonight to show you that I'm housebroken and everything," he threatened jokingly.

"Evan asked Donna to move in with him."

That was obviously news to Blackie. He released her. "How do you feel about it? Not long ago you weren't sure if Donna was good for Evan."

"She is, though. I don't see any reason they shouldn't live together. What do you think?"

"I hope she doesn't distract him too much and interfere with the recording," Blackie said. Then he shook his head, dismissing his reservation. "I think their living together will be okay. I agree with you that she's good for Evan."

That surprised Rachel, and her reaction was not lost on Blackie.

"Don't look so shocked. I'm not against certain domestic arrangements."

No, he probably wouldn't object to shacking up for a while. It would be convenient as long as he was interested in the woman.

"What's wrong?"

"Nothing, except I believe that there's a little more to their relationship than cohabitation for the duration of the . . . um . . . attraction between them."

Blackie was so astonished by Rachel's statement that he made no attempt to detain her. He watched her head for the club, where Evan was waiting for her. What had he said to upset her? She obviously had nothing against two people living together, but when he said he didn't either, her mood plunged lower than the deepest blues lament.

He watched father and daughter approach him, Evan's arm around Rachel's shoulders. "I'm sorry you have to rush off, sugar," Evan said. "Are you sure you can't stay for a while?"

"Positive. I haven't eaten in so long, my stomach is sending out distress signals." As if on cue, her stomach rumbled loudly enough to be heard, and Rachel apologized.

"There's an all-night deli up the street," Blackie said. "I'll take you there. If I'm not back in time," he told Evan, "start with the couple of numbers you can do without me." Blackie took Rachel's arm and propelled her authoritatively toward the door.

Rachel started to object, but her own father cut her off.

"No problem," Evan called after them.

"I can get my own food," Rachel pointed out curtly.

"Of course you can," Blackie agreed amiably. "But I'd just as soon not have you walk here at night alone."

In her high-heeled shoes Rachel had trouble keeping up with Blackie's long-legged stride. "Are we rushing to a fire?" she snapped.

"Sorry," he said, and he slowed down. "I'm still pumped up by the music. What did you think of my new composition?"

"The revival-beat piece? It was great. I suspect most of the audience wanted to jump up and shout and sway to the rhythm."

"Did you want to do that?"

"Yes."

Her answer pleased him enormously, and he too wanted to jump up and shout, but he restrained himself. He sensed that Rachel's anger was dissipating, and that made him glad too.

When they entered the deli, Blackie called to the man behind the counter, "Sid, bring us two vegetarian specials and two bottles of mineral water." Without waiting for Rachel's consent, he led her to a back booth.

"My, my. We're high-handed tonight, aren't we? Masterful, even," Rachel said, hearing the sarcasm in her voice and not liking it.

"You left me no choice."

"I left you no choice?" she demanded.

"That's right. Every so often you get contrary, and there's no reasoning with you," he stated. "You suddenly climb up on your high horse, flash those cool eyes, and just dare me to come near you."

"I do no such thing," Rachel denied hotly.

"You just did a few minutes ago. The only difference is, tonight I'm not letting you get away with it."

Sid brought two grilled-cheese sandwiches accompanied by an avocado-almond salad. Rachel had decided to protest Blackie's ridiculous claims by refusing to eat, but the enticing aroma and her growling stomach wouldn't obey her pride. She ate half a sandwich before she said another word.

"This is good," she murmured, digging into the salad.

Blackie tried carefully to keep his self-satisfied reaction from showing. He didn't quite succeed.

When Rachel's hunger was assuaged, she said, "Don't look so smug. It's not one of the more attractive emotions."

The pseudo-meek expression replacing his smugness didn't fool her either. "Okay, so I was grumpy because I was half-starved. I give you credit for figuring that out."

"Thank you." His voice was still meek, but his blue eyes glowed with amusement and affection. "Now that you're fed and no longer as mean as a picked-up snake, why did you get angry when I agreed that living together was okay?"

Rachel sipped some mineral water to give her time to think. "Because I'm sure we'd list different reasons for it."

"Would we? Tell me why Evan and Donna should live together."

"Because they're mature and know what they need.

They need each other. They like and respect each other. They share real affection."

"I'm surprised you didn't mention the operative word women always use."

"What's that?" Rachel demanded.

"Love."

"I don't know if they do love each other. I didn't ask, and they didn't volunteer the information."

"You don't think love is necessary for people to live together?" Blackie asked.

Of course it was. Rachel wouldn't consider living with a man unless she loved him. Actually, she wouldn't consider living with a man unless she was married to him. That, however, she wouldn't tell Blackie. Not when there were those almost taunting undercurrents in his voice and that challenging, arrogant expression on his face.

"Since I've never lived with a man I wasn't married to, and since I never intend to, I've had no reason to consider what is or isn't necessary. It's absolutely not an option I'd ever consider."

Blackie's eyebrows arched. "Never say never. You're wrong about me, you know."

"Wrong?"

"Dead wrong." He raised her hand to his mouth and kissed each finger.

She felt each kiss sizzle all the way to her toes. Her voice squeaked a little when she finally rallied her wits to ask, "Wrong about what?"

"That I consider physical attraction a sufficient basis

for living together." His hands shot up to her arms, and he pulled her halfway across the table between them to claim her mouth in a hungry, demanding kiss. He released her as abruptly as he'd reached for her. They looked at each other speechlessly.

He dropped some bills onto the table, draped an arm around her shoulders, waved to Sid, and walked her back to her car.

Neither of them spoke. What was there to say, Rachel brooded. Much too much—and not nearly enough—had already been said.

Blackie took her car keys from her and unlocked the driver's door. He closed it courteously when she was seated. "Drive carefully."

Their dinner had been a success, Rachel thought, a small satisfied smile on her lips. Carefully she divided the smidgen of leftover seafood casserole into the dishes of the three cats, who milled around her legs expectantly.

"Amazing," Blackie muttered, watching.

"What is? The cats, because they like leftovers?"

"No, because they waited so patiently in the hall all evening, yet now look at them go at it."

"They're polite. Besides, patience is an inborn trait of cats. Haven't you ever seen one sit for hours in front of a mouse hole?"

"Can't say that I have." Blackie transferred his gaze from the feasting cats to their mistress, who was stretching to reach the top shelf of a cupboard. He stopped himself just in time from offering to help her. Instead he leaned back against the counter and watched the graceful lines of her body with pleasure.

"I think it was great of Donna to offer her services as vocalist at the auction," Rachel said. "Don't you agree?"

Not hearing an answer, she turned to look at him. As she met his hot-eyed gaze, her breath stilled for a second before it rushed out with redoubled force. Her heart was behaving in a similarly idiotic manner, she observed.

Blackie crossed the kitchen and kissed her. Slow, lingering kisses, carefully paced, carefully containing the passion that made both of them tremble.

Rachel pulled back, breathless. She shook her head.

"I know it's too soon. The melody isn't quite right yet," he murmured.

"You're not angry?" she asked.

"It would be foolish to be angry and useless besides. It's like getting angry because the strawberries aren't ripe yet or because it didn't snow on Christmas morning. Some things are out of our control. We can't hurry them. If we do, we'll ruin everything."

Rachel looked at him, surprised and pleased.

"Do you think I'm crazy?"

"No. I think you're an extraordinary man."

"Don't look at me quite so sweetly," he warned, "or I'll forget all my principles and take a chance on ruining it for us."

"In that case, I'll escort you to my door."

Chapter Ten

"Do you understand what that man is saying?" Peggy whispered, inclining her head toward the stage.

Listening to the auctioneer's rhythmic, running patter intently, Rachel said, "Not really. Just the sum of money that's been bid." They were standing on the sidelines, watching the proceedings with interest.

"Excuse me, Peggy," Rachel murmured. "Time to circulate."

She moved outside, where refreshment booths were set up alongside the entrance to the pavilion where the animals were on display. Placing the food temptingly where people had to pass the animals ready to be adopted had been a stroke of genius, Rachel thought again.

In the brilliant afternoon light her gaze flew to the gazebo. The transport team Blackie had hired to deliver the piano was setting it up according to Evan's directions. Poco fussed with his drums while Blackie and

Jawbone engaged in a serious discussion. Everything looked fine.

Handsome Justin Emil, a veterinarian's assistant, was on hand to answer questions on the care of pets. That too had been a stroke of genius, judging by the crowd of women around his table.

"How're we doing?" Rachel asked Seth.

He rose and flashed her one of his rare smiles. "Splendidly," he said, patting the cash box. Leaning toward Rachel with an air of confidentiality, he said, "Do you know we had one guy pick four pets? Two dogs and two cats. Imagine that."

"That's great." Then a worried look crossed Rachel's face. "He wasn't weird or anything, was he? I mean, you did check him out, right?"

Seth drew himself up to his full five feet six inches. "Of course I did. Checked his driver's license, wrote down his place of employment, and asked for references."

"Good, good," Rachel soothed.

"He drives a Porsche." Clearly feeling vindicated, Seth sat down and fussily rearranged the remaining adoption forms.

"Good job," Rachel repeated, and she hurried off.

"We're going to need all the volunteers we can scare up to retrieve our pet carriers," Dorothy told her.

Most people were only too happy to leave a five-dollar deposit in exchange for the carriers. It made transporting their new pet so much easier.

"I'll help. We'll get them back. Don't worry," Rachel

said. Slowly she walked through the pavilion, stopping frequently to admire and speak to the animals.

"Hi there, handsome," she said to a huge, sleepy-eyed, gray-striped tiger tomcat.

"I keep hoping you'll say that to me sometime."

Rachel looked up, meeting the smiling brown eyes of Justin Emil. "Hi there, handsome," she teased.

Who was the man talking to Rachel, Blackie wondered. The guy was entirely too good-looking to be smiling like that at her. Jealousy, as intense as it was unexpected, slashed through him. Here he was, trying to impress her, while she smiled at some blond Adonis. That's not how it was supposed to go, he reflected, aggrieved.

"Sign here, Mr. Madigan."

One of the deliverymen thrust a clipboard at him. "Why? You aren't leaving, are you? We'll be through in less than an hour, and you can take the piano right back."

"Well, I don't know . . ." the uniformed man said, scratching his head.

"It doesn't make sense to fight traffic, then turn around to come back as soon as you get to the garage." Blackie knew if he let the men leave, they wouldn't be back for hours. "Why don't you go get some refreshments? Look at the animals. Pick out one, and I'll pay for it."

"Yeah? My kid's been pestering me about getting a dog. I might just take you up on your offer," the man said. "Okay. We'll stick around."

Rachel was still with that guy. He glowered at them

ferociously, but mental telepathy didn't work. He'd have to break them up and remind that gray-eyed beauty whose woman she was. He reached for his sax.

At the sound of the first phrase, Rachel turned as if an invisible rope pulled her. The lilting tone lured her with an unbreakable force.

"Excuse me," she muttered distractedly, her gaze fastened on Blackie. Almost like a sleepwalker she moved toward the musician, leaving the veterinarian standing there with an astonished look on his face.

Blackie continued to play his Pied Piper theme, watching Rachel's approach. When she was close enough to touch, he stopped.

"Don't quit," Rachel protested. "That was beautiful."

Beautiful enough to get her away from Mr. Handsome. "Who was that guy with you?"

"What guy? Oh, Justin Emil. He's a veterinarian's assistant. He helps with the animals."

Okay. He couldn't remember ever feeling possessive of any woman. Why that should surprise him, he didn't know. Where Rachel was concerned, everything he did was uncharacteristic.

"You look lovely."

"Thank you."

"How's the auction going?" Blackie took her hand and led her a few steps away from the gazebo for privacy.

Rachel crossed her fingers. "Okay, so far. It's funny what people will bid on. I suppose one man's trash *is* another man's treasure. Lucky for us."

"And the animals?"

"According to Seth we're doing 'splendidly.' " Rachel mimicked Seth's somewhat squeaky voice perfectly.

They grinned at each other.

"Are you going to convince Evan to get a pet?" Blackie asked.

The grin faded from Rachel's face. "I'd love to, but it might not be fair to the animal. What if Evan has to go back into rehab? Animals get attached to people."

Blackie put his arms around her comfortingly. "I'm sorry. I didn't mean to put a damper on your day."

"You didn't." Rachel forced a smile onto her face. "Have you been in the auction hall yet?"

"No. But I'll bid on something for you. What would you like?"

"Well . . . promise you won't laugh?"

"I won't ever laugh at you. With you, but not at you."

"There's a music box with a couple dancing on top when it's wound up. It plays something dreadfully schmaltzy like 'The Tennessee Waltz,' but I kind of like it." She watched his face closely.

With supreme effort, Blackie controlled his facial muscles. Not even the corners of his mouth twitched. Rachel might be a high-powered executive, but there was a gentle, kind, sentimental streak in her a mile wide. Strays and hurt animals. Musicians with problems. Sentimental music boxes. This gray-eyed woman was complex. Complex and wonderful. The kind of woman you kept. Startled by this unorthodox thought, Blackie scratched his beard.

"If you think its too silly . . ." Rachel began.

"No, it's not too silly. I'll get the box for you. When does it come up on the block?"

Rachel glanced at the list she held. "Anytime now. We'll have to hurry. You'll have to register and get a bidding paddle."

Blackie grabbed her by the hand, and like children they ran all the way to the hall. He registered, then, armed with a numbered paddle, they joined the sizable crowd. Bidding with panache, Blackie managed to drive up the price of the music box.

Rachel plucked his sleeve to get his attention. "Don't bid any higher, please," she begged softly when the auctioneer said forty dollars.

"But that's the object of the auction. To raise money," he reminded her, lifting the paddle again.

"You might get stuck with an exorbitant price."

Rachel was really worried about his finances, Blackie realized, and he experienced a pang of guilt. This, however, wasn't the time for a major disclosure. "Don't worry. I won't bankrupt myself." He managed to drive the bid up to seventy dollars. "Darn. I hoped to get it up to a hundred," he murmured, disappointed.

Rachel heaved a sigh of relief.

Blackie presented the music box to her with a flourish.

"Thank you. I love it," she said, "even though it's gaudier than I expected it to'be." She smiled at him brilliantly. "I'll leave it in the office for now."

He followed her into the empty office. Carefully she placed the box on the desk. "Do we have time to play it once?" she asked.

He glanced at his watch. "Sure."

When the sentimental music filled the room, he bowed and asked Rachel to dance. He waltzed her around the office expertly. When the box wound down, his arms tightened around her. She willingly lifted her face for his kiss.

Odd, he thought, while thinking was still possible, their kisses were never the same.

Odd, he thought, he didn't think he'd ever get tired of kissing this woman.

The noise of people leaving the hall for refreshments pulled them back to reality. "I think it's time for the official entertainment to start," Rachel reminded him.

"Will I see you later?"

"When?"

"After the auction is over."

"I have to help transport the unclaimed animals back to the shelter. I won't be through with all this for quite a while."

"I don't mind how late it gets, just so I can be with you."

"Okay, but now we've got to get back, or Evan will send out a search party."

With his arm around her shoulders, they walked back to the gazebo.

"Sugar, turn Blackie loose. We need him," Evan called to her.

"You heard him. Go."

"I'll play for you, Rachel."

* * *

As the group launched into the first set, people gathered around. Blackie's sax, smooth and deep as black velvet, slid over Rachel with its customary bewitching magic. She leaned against the trunk of a nearby tree and lost herself in the music. They played one of Evan's new compositions, showing off his mastery of the two-handed tremolo, which soared into an explosive eruption of sound.

Donna sang "Our Love Is Here to Stay" and "I Didn't Know What Time It Was." Listening closely to the lyrics, Rachel trembled. They could have been written for her. The mountains might indeed crumble in time, but she would never not care about that sexy, beguiling horn man.

Blast him. It wasn't fair. She'd fought so hard against falling for him. Useless, useless. Rachel closed her eyes in agony.

As if Blackie sensed the struggle in her, his sax cut loose with a soaring ululation whose power and beauty penetrated to her bone marrow.

Laura, elegant in a beige linen suit, joined Rachel. "Seeing and listening to your sax man, I understand why you're attracted to him," she said, her voice soft. "If music imitates feelings and emotions, then he's got a lot to offer you."

"I know."

"You'll have to decide if that outweighs the negative aspects of a musician's life. No one can do that for you."

Rachel nodded. "I know, and it scares me to death."

"Difficult decisions are always frightening. There are no guarantees that you've made the right one."

"No guarantees of a happily ever after," Rachel murmured.

"That you have to work at."

"Even you and Harley?" Rachel asked, a little surprised. She'd always thought of their marriage as the perfect one.

"Yes, even us."

"I suppose if people were perfect, they wouldn't have to work on relationships."

"No, they wouldn't, but think how boring that would be. No arguments. No reconciliations. Just placid agreements and bland harmony."

They lapsed into silence, listening to the music. If Blackie were perfect, Rachel mused, his music wouldn't grip her the way it did. It wouldn't be tinged with the darker tones that hinted at pain, danger, and plaintive needs.

The crowd around the gazebo, easily tripled in size by now, applauded enthusiastically.

"Have you been inside yet?" Rachel asked.

"No. I was hoping I could give you a donation and skip the auction."

"What? And miss your chance to bid on a pink flamingo for your lawn or a lamp in the shape of a hula dancer?" Rachel teased.

The women smiled at each other.

"We'll give your donation to Seth," Rachel said, and she led the way.

* * *

Hours later only members of the committee and the cleanup crew were left.

Seth tallied the checks and the cash while Rachel looked at the animals they had to take back to the shelter. There really weren't that many, she noted, pleased.

"Seth? Seth? Old One-Eye is gone!" Rachel exclaimed. "Did someone adopt him?"

"Yes."

"Oh, my stars. Did you tell them that he's old and blind in one eye?"

Seth raised his gaze from his calculator to look at Rachel. "Of course I did," he said testily. "I wouldn't lie."

"I didn't mean to imply that you would. It's just so amazing that someone would adopt a half-blind old tomcat."

"It was the guy I told you about. The one who took two dogs and two cats."

"Well, bless him," Rachel said. "I'll remember him in my prayers."

"This is strange," Seth said, blinking bewilderedly through his wire-rimmed glasses.

"What is?" Rachel asked.

"This cashier's check. I don't remember anybody giving it to me."

"Well, you were busy and might not have noticed it."

"Not notice a check for ten thousand dollars?" Seth's expression was one of injured outrage.

"Ten thousand? Are you sure there are that many

zeroes?" Rachel walked around the table to look at the check.

"I'm not likely to make that kind of error. I'm a banker, for heaven's sake."

"Sorry. It's just so unbelievable," Rachel said. "Who's it from?"

"The only name on a cashier's check is that of the recipient." Seth sounded like an exasperatedly patient teacher speaking to a particularly dense student.

"That's right. He or she didn't wait for a receipt?"

"No."

Rachel studied the cashier's check in wonder. "Bless him or her." She blew a kiss at the check.

Blackie reluctantly attended a meeting at Obsidian International. Odd, once upon a time the company had been his whole life, yet now he tried to get out of meetings.

"You really should study the report on one of your new companies. I don't know much about the beauty business, but this doesn't look right to me," Ben complained.

"If something's wrong, fix it. I don't have time to look at the report now." Changing the subject, Blackie asked, "How do you like your new pet, Ben?"

Ben snorted. "The fluffy little devil wakes me up every morning by purring into my ear. He attacks the dust mop as if it were a giant mouse, and he's systematically shredding the dining room curtains."

"As I remember, those curtains were ugly anyway,"

Blackie said, unmoved. He signed the contracts page by page.

"How's the little terrier I gave you as part of your bonus for working extra hours while I'm in the studio?" he asked his assistant.

For a moment Curtis seemed to be at a loss for words. "Chester's okay," he finally said, "except he's got a thing for my wife's slippers."

Blackie looked up from the contract, waiting.

"Chews them up," Curtis added.

"Ah. Perfectly normal. He's a growing puppy and needs to exercise his teeth," Blackie pronounced with the air of an authority. He remembered Seth's saying something like that to him. He'd given the other dog to his second assistant. "How's George getting along with his pet?"

"Says he's lost five pounds already. The dog is part hound and doesn't know the meaning of walking. He runs, pulling George behind him, trying desperately to hang on to the leash," Curtis said, attempting to hide his gleeful satisfaction. Chewed slippers, by comparison, seemed a bargain.

"That's great. George has been putting on weight lately," Blackie said, his voice hearty. "There, that should do it." He handed the contracts to Curtis, who hurried off before he could be presented with another live gift.

"What's gotten into you, brother?" Ben demanded. "What's with this sudden interest in animal protection?"

"Animals have as much right to live as we do."

"Yes, I agree, but—" Ben broke off and studied his brother carefully. "There's more to this than meets the eye." A knowing, triumphant look spread across his face. "There's a woman involved, isn't there?"

A brief flicker in Blackie's eyes confirmed his suspicions. Ben slapped his thigh and roared with laughter. When he'd controlled his outburst, he said, "Oh, how the mighty have fallen. It does my heart good to see the king of the unbelievers caught in the web of love."

Blackie looked at his brother coldly. "Don't be ridiculous. I'm not in love. How could I be, when I'm not sure such a thing exists outside the heads of a few romantics?"

Even as he made this claim, Blackie knew he protested too much. Besides, he was no longer sure that there wasn't such a thing as romantic love. His emotions were all over the place.

"Of course you're not in love." Ben's voice dripped with teasing sarcasm. "Next you'll tell me there isn't a woman either."

"There's a woman," Blackie conceded with ill grace. "She's special. I'll admit to a strong physical attraction between us, but that's all."

"Uh-huh." Ben stressed the second syllable, nodding his head. "Physical attraction," he repeated, obviously not buying it.

"You've heard of it?" Blackie snapped.

"Sure." Seeing that his brother was as testy as a shedding rattlesnake, Ben refrained from saying anything else, but his expression spoke volumes. He merely grinned and left, closing the door firmly. When he heard an object hit the door, he laughed delightedly.

Blackie crossed to the door to retrieve the shoe he'd hurled after his brother, angry that he'd let Ben get to him. Couldn't a man be attracted to a woman without having his feelings labeled?

Rachel glanced at the building. This was the first time Blackie had invited her to his place, warning her not to expect too much, as he'd moved into the loft only a few weeks ago.

From the outside the building looked as if it had been a small production plant of some sort. Now the tall windows had been outfitted with thermopane glass, and someone had placed colored fleur-de-lis panels into the windows next to the main entrance.

Blackie must have been watching for her, because he flung the door wide open and pulled her into his arms for an enthusiastic hug.

"Let me show you the place."

He led her into a high-ceilinged room that was divided into two main areas by green steel scaffolding-like structures. Matchstick blinds separated the bath and bedroom from the rest of the loft. The hi-tech look was softened by gleaming hardwood floors and numerous plants crowded around the tall windows. The far end of the room featured a galley kitchen, an eating counter, and four bamboo bar stools.

Rachel walked slowly through the room, noting the comfortable, upholstered chairs circled into a conversation group, touching the keys of the upright piano that dominated the music area. Hundreds of records and tapes, filed chronologically by genre, were arranged on shelves along the wall. The computer on the desk seemed out of place in the room. Rachel stopped in front of it and turned to Blackie with a questioning look.

"That's part of my day job," he explained, turning her away from it. Gesturing toward the room, he asked, "Well, what do you think of it?"

"I like it. I always thought a loft would be a messy jumble of things, but yours is arranged very functionally and neatly. At the same time it isn't cold. I think it's the bright colors and the wood and the plants and . . ." Movement in front of one of the windows through which warm sunlight streamed caught her eye. In a large, fur-lined basket between two Schefflera plants a huge black-and-white cat stretched leisurely. Rachel's breath caught.

"Old One-Eye?" she murmured, walking slowly toward him. He sat with that unique, complete dignity achieved only by very old cats. She dropped onto her knees before him. He allowed her to stroke his massive, silky head for a few seconds before he curled up contentedly for another snooze.

Rachel stood up and turned toward Blackie. Her throat felt tight with such happiness that she couldn't speak. Wordlessly she hugged him fiercely, lovingly. Blackie held her, stroking her hair. When she could, she pulled back to look into his eyes. "Why?" she asked.

Blackie shrugged. "I don't know. We looked at each other, and something clicked. His purrs harmonize with

some of the lower notes on my sax. It's uncanny. He knows when I hit a note that's not exactly right. Old Cy is my severest critic."

"Old Cy? Don't tell me you named him Cyclops?" Rachel laughed, unable to help herself.

"Why not? It's no worse than Old One-Eye."

"No, I guess not. His being a stray, we never knew what he'd been named as a kitten." Still smiling, she curled her fingers into his dark beard. Then she remembered. "Seth said that the man who bought Old One-Eye also adopted three other animals." She looked at him expectantly.

"Uh-huh. All three are placed with loving people, being spoiled and fussed over. I'll take you to visit them if you like."

A surge of intense feelings jolted Rachel. She tightened her arms around Blackie, pressing her face against his warm throat. "Is it any wonder that I . . . I like you so?" Quickly she turned away before she could reveal anything more damaging.

"Let me check to see how the coffee is doing," Blackie said, guessing Rachel needed some space.

Rachel wandered through the loft, stopping before the computer, which was a newer, more expensive model than the one she used at Athena. Beside it lay a beautifully designed brochure about a company called Obsidian International. The name was unfamiliar to Rachel, but that meant nothing, since she concentrated strictly on cosmetics companies.

That reminded her of Exotica and the disturbing fact

that their sleazy competitor was about to launch Amore. As always when she thought of Exotica, her stomach knotted in anxiety, but she vowed not to let business ruin this visit.

"Coffee's ready." Blackie set two mugs onto the counter.

Rachel joined him. "Is Obsidian the company you work for? I saw their brochure by the computer," she added when she noticed his startled expression.

Somewhat warily Blackie admitted that it was.

Blackie debated with himself. He hadn't wanted to reveal his other persona until he was sure Rachel wouldn't walk out on him when he told her, but this seemed such a natural opportunity that he decided to risk it. Mentally crossing his fingers, he began, "I design computer programs."

"You do? Good heavens! Isn't that light-years away from music?"

"Not really. Both are based on precise mathematical schemata."

Her gray eyes watched him intently, trustingly. Blackie prayed that they'd still be that trusting when he finished his confession.

The telephone shrilled, making both of them jump a little.

When Blackie hesitated, Rachel said, "Don't tell me you're one of those people who can resist a ringing phone."

He merely grinned at her.

Rachel watched him walk to the telephone, admiring

his lithe movements. At first she didn't listen—not until Blackie's responses grew terse, and Evan's name was mentioned.

It couldn't be happening again, she thought, dread settling into her stomach like a lead weight. Evan had been doing so well. Rachel stood up, waiting, leaning against the back of the stool to support her trembling legs.

Blackie hung up. "That was Donna. Evan didn't come home after last night's gig." As he looked at Rachel, he saw all color drain from her face. She swayed slightly. "Honey, it doesn't have to be bad news," he said, hurrying to her side. He put his arms around her and held her. Her body was rigid.

"Did Evan say anything to you last night? Was he upset?" Her wide gray eyes, filled with fear and worry, looked at him pleadingly.

At that moment Blackie would have gladly traded his wealth for an answer that would chase the terror from Rachel's eyes.

"Evan was off talking to Jawbone, so we only nodded to each other as I left." He thought for a moment, trying to picture the scene. "I don't think Evan was upset, though Jawbone might have been. What usually triggers Evan's binges?"

"Anything. Everything. Nothing." Rachel slumped against Blackie, the rigidity draining from her body.

He held her, smoothing her hair. He wasn't sure he didn't prefer the rigidity to this defeated despair that gripped her. "Rachel, we don't know what happened, so let's not imagine the worst."

"I know," she murmured, "but it's hard not to. It usually starts this way. He doesn't come home when he's supposed to."

Rachel remembered all the times she had watched from the window, the many trips she'd made outside, looking up and down the street, willing Evan to come home, all the nights she had slept fitfully on the sofa, waking up every hour to check his bedroom, praying to find him there, asleep. Then searching countless bars after school or work, trying to find him and rarely succeeding. He had an uncanny knack for eluding her when he skidded into one of his alcoholic sprees. This time she had allowed herself to build such hopes for him that the possibility of a relapse tore her apart.

In a small, shaky voice she said, "If he doesn't make it this time, with all he's got going for him, he never will. I'm not sure I can go through this again."

The pain and despair in her voice sliced right through Blackie's heart. He cradled her face with gentle hands. "This time you don't have to go through it alone. I'll be with you every step of the way." When Rachel didn't say anything but only stared at him, wide-eyed, he added, "I swear I'll be right beside you all the time."

Rachel rarely cried, but the enormity of Blackie's offer brought tears to her eyes. With a superhuman effort she fought them down. "No one's ever offered to stand by me," she whispered. "No one. Not in all the years I've fought Evan's demons."

"From now on we'll fight together."

For such a simple statement, it carried a tremendous emotional punch that left Rachel trembling.

"It's okay to cry," Blackie said softly, and he wrapped his arms securely around her.

"I know," she murmured against his chest, but she did not weep. She seldom allowed herself the luxury of tears, in part because she feared it would rob her of the strength she needed to deal with Evan's drinking, and in part because she feared that once she started to cry, she wouldn't be able to stop. "Being held like this beats tears any day."

"I can hold you forever," Blackie said. He kissed her hair, inhaling its lovely fragrance.

Rachel took a couple of deep, shuddering breaths. "I never know what to do," she confessed. "Sit by the phone or go out and search the bars. Maybe Jawbone knows something. He doesn't have a phone, but I've got his address." Clutching at this slim hope, Rachel grabbed her purse and rummaged through it, searching for her address book. "Here it is."

Blackie looked at it. "We'll take the Dan Ryan going south and exit at Eighty-seventh Street."

The idea of action, any action, was infinitely preferable to waiting, Rachel thought. When the phone rang again, her heart hammered with anxiety. Her gaze fastened unwaveringly on to Blackie's face as he answered the phone.

"When?" she heard him ask.

"That's a relief. Rachel is here with me. Which hospital?"

Hospital? Rachel clutched Blackie's arm in alarm.

"Evan's okay," Blackie said even before he finished hanging up. "He phoned Donna from Cook County Hospital. Jawbone's been hurt. Slipped and twisted his ankle, but it isn't broken. He's going to be all right."

"Thank God." Rachel leaned into Blackie, her body going limp with relief.

"Apparently Evan spent most of what was left of the night and this morning trying to keep Jawbone from falling off the wagon. Something about his wife's showing up. I didn't know Jawbone was married."

"Maybelle! That awful woman has jerked him around for years!" Rachel exclaimed. She shook her head. "I don't mean to be hateful, but that Maybelle is something else. I've never understood why Jawbone keeps taking her back. Surely he doesn't still love her after all she's put him through."

"Don't look to me for the answer. Human relationships rarely make sense to me. Do you feel better now?"

"Oh, yes. I don't know what I would have done without you."

"Coped. The way you always have in the past. You're a strong woman, Rachel Carradine."

"Maybe. But do you know what it meant to me to hear you offer to stay? To share my worries?"

"I was glad to do it. Why wouldn't I?"

Rachel shrugged. None of the other musicians she'd known over the years had offered to help, not even her ex-husband.

"Let's take my car," she said.

Chapter Eleven

"This time Exotica has gone too far," Sam Thornton said, dropping a folder onto Rachel's desk. "We're going to sue them."

"We are?" Rachel looked through the various items in the folder, which included Exotica's ads for Amore. "Can we win?"

"I wouldn't suggest we sue if I didn't think so."

"Good. We've been wanting to do that for years."

Sam pulled his earlobe, a gesture he used when something puzzled him. "Funny thing is, I could have sworn the new owner would have made Exotica clean up its act. I've met the president of Obsidian International, and Madigan struck me as a decent sort of guy."

Madigan? It couldn't be, was Rachel's first thought, but how many Madigans could one company have? Grasping the edge of her desk, she swallowed convulsively. She had to try twice before her voice functioned enough for her to ask, "Madigan? What's his first name?"

"Let me see." The attorney took a sheet from the folder and looked at it. "Blackstone."

She had meant to ask Blackie what his real name was but hadn't gotten around to it, just as they had never gotten back to discussing his job at Obsidian. She held out a hand for the sheet. The letters swam before her eyes, causing her to close them briefly. *Blackstone J. Madigan.* Part of her mind refused to believe that this could be Blackie. Her Blackie. The man she loved. It simply couldn't be.

"Can you describe Madigan?" she asked, bracing herself for Sam's answer.

He looked surprised but answered her question. "He's brilliant. I guess in his field he's some kind of genius. That's how he got to be a millionaire by age twenty-five."

"What does he look like?" Rachel asked through bloodless lips.

"He's tall. Dark hair and beard. Blue eyes. I guess women would consider him handsome."

They would. She had and did. Rachel heard Sam's voice drone on, but his words didn't penetrate her milling thoughts. The whole room seemed to be swaying and swirling.

"Are you all right?"

"No." She would never be all right again. Nothing would ever be all right again. Blackie owned Exotica. "I'm going to be sick," she murmured, and she rushed to the bathroom.

Later, as she bathed her face with cold water, she thought she had never been so violently sick to her stomach in her entire life. It was as if her body, by rejecting the food she had consumed, was trying to reject the devastating information that had infused her brain like a virulent virus.

Rachel remembered Peggy's knocking on the door but didn't recall getting her handbag or taking the elevator to the parking garage. She stared at her car, not knowing what to do first. Perhaps it was all a misunderstanding, a mistake. She would go to Blackie's loft and ask him. No, he wouldn't be there. At least she didn't think so. The recording session didn't start until the afternoon, he had told her.

Was it only two days ago that he had offered his support, as if she were important to him? Acute pain gripped Rachel's heart as if an iron hand were squeezing it. She gasped, forcing herself to breathe deeply to lessen the pain.

If he really was president of Obsidian, he would be at his office. Using her cell phone, she asked Peggy to look up the address. The offices of Obsidian were only a few blocks away, a distance she could cover on foot in minutes. Suddenly Rachel had to know the truth, no matter what it was.

The corporate offices of Obsidian International were on the fifteenth floor. There an attractive receptionist informed Rachel that Mr. Madigan saw no one without an appointment.

"I'm Rachel Carradine. He will see me."

Something in Rachel's pale but determined face caused the woman to reconsider. She murmured something into the telephone. "Mr. Madigan will see you. Last door on the left."

Blackie met her in his antechamber, slipping into his suit coat. She looked at him as if he were a stranger. "It's true, isn't it? You look every inch the company president, and even if you didn't, the guilt on your face would give you away."

"I meant to tell you—really I did. On Saturday I started to, but then Donna called, and after that it slipped my mind."

"Slipped your mind?" she asked, her voice incredulous.

"Just as it slipped yours that you were second in command at Athena."

That hit home. Rachel was silent for a moment. Then she said, "If that were all, I could forgive you, even understand it, but this other thing is unforgivable."

"Rachel, what are you talking about? What other thing? What are you accusing me of?" For the first time Blackie recognized Rachel's distraught state, and alarm knifed through him. "What's this all about?"

"Don't pretend you don't know!"

"I don't. I swear I haven't so much as looked at another woman since the evening we met."

"But you still betrayed me. If it had been with another woman, it wouldn't hurt so much, because it wouldn't have been so cold-bloodedly planned."

Blackie grasped her shoulders with his hands. "Rachel, spit it out. How have I betrayed you?"

"I swore no man would ever get at Athena again through me, but you managed it beautifully. I never even suspected you. You were so clever, I bought your jazzman act and never asked what else you did. I can't believe I fell for you when I knew so little about you. I can't believe I was that dumb. But don't celebrate your cleverness too soon. We're suing Exotica for every penny they stole from us."

Blackie's eyebrows drew together in a fierce frown. "Exotica?"

Angrily Rachel shook his hands from her shoulders. "Stop pretending you don't own that sleazy company."

At last Blackie had a dim glimmer of what Rachel was so upset about. "So that's what Ben was trying to talk to me about."

"You and I are on opposite sides. I don't ever want to see you or talk to you again." With that she turned from him and started toward the door.

"You can't mean that!" Blackie cried out. "Rachel, wait."

"Don't touch me," she hissed. "Haven't you done me enough harm?"

Blackie realized she was too upset to listen to anything he had to say. "I'll talk to you when I've found out what's going on. But we're not through, Rachel. We've just begun. Remember that."

A tortured sob escaped her throat. Pressing a fist against her mouth, she ran out of the office, past the astonished receptionist, and past the elevator to the stairwell.

Blackie started after her but stopped himself. First he had to find out what had happened. "Get Ben in here!" he bellowed. "And George and Curtis. On the double."

His secretary stared at him, openmouthed. In the ten years she had worked for Blackstone Madigan, he had never raised his voice.

"Now," he snapped.

"Yes, sir." She snatched up the telephone receiver with alacrity.

Blackie paced, too agitated to do anything else.

Ben was the first to arrive.

"How in the hell did I end up owning Exotica?"

"That's the cosmetics company I've been trying to talk to you about."

"Next time rope and hog-tie me to make me listen. We're going to be sued by Athena Cosmetics."

"I'm not surprised."

"That's not the worst of it. It might cost me the woman I'm interested in. I can't allow that. I won't."

Ben raised an eyebrow at the word *interested,* which he thought an understatement, but refrained from commenting.

The two assistants arrived and soon left with instructions to find out everything they could about Exotica. Blackie called a luncheon meeting to plan their course of action.

"Fill me in on what you know about Exotica," he told Ben. When his brother finished, Blackie's face was ashen. "No wonder Rachel doesn't want to see me again. How in the world did we end up with such a crooked outfit?" He strode to the window and stared out. "One thing's clear. I've got to delegate most of my responsibilities here at Obsidian to other people."

From the Exotica debacle it was obvious to Blackie that he couldn't be both a musician and the head of a company. It was too much. Although he had thoroughly enjoyed building Obsidian International, it no longer satisfied him. Not the way his music did. It was time to make a complete career and life change.

Rachel walked without a destination, oblivious to the people in the street. A sudden rain shower brought her back to reality. She found herself sitting on a bench in Grant Park. Raising her face to the rain, she wept without restraint. Even if anyone was watching her, her tears would be indistinguishable from the raindrops. Sometime later she walked to the parking garage to retrieve her car and drove home.

She dropped her sodden clothes to the bathroom floor. Even standing under a hot shower didn't warm her up. Wrapping herself into a terry cloth robe and a quilt, she curled up on her bed, exhausted, broken-hearted, without a shred of hope or comfort.

The telephone rang repeatedly, insistently, but she ignored it, feeling she had neither the strength nor the inclination to talk to anyone, least of all Blackie. One of those persistent callers had to be he. She just knew it. She could picture him scowling at the receiver, willing her to answer the phone. How he must have laughed at her not very subtle efforts to protect his meager bank account. She cringed.

For the hundredth time she asked herself how she could have been so mistaken about him. She could have sworn on a stack of Bibles that he was straight and honest. The thought that she had made such a fundamental error in judging someone severely dented her self-confidence. Her ability to judge people was one of the qualities that made her a good executive. Perhaps she had lost the talent and was washed up. Not that she cared, hurting as she did.

She should have known better. Blackie was a musician. That alone should have been enough to put him off-limits. She had tried not to fall in love with him. She really had. It hadn't worked.

Sometime during the endless night she dozed off briefly. At three she awoke, and for a brief, exhilarating second she didn't remember what had happened. Then, realizing that the man she loved was lost to her, she burst into sobs that shook her body as if she were in the grip of some dreadful seizure.

Somehow she got through the next day. She spent long hours in the lab, working on the cologne she was designing for men. But even there thoughts of Blackie plagued her. She had started work on the cologne because of him, planning to call it Crescendo. Late in the afternoon Sam called her.

"I got some astonishing news. Exotica has pulled all its advertising on Amore. There has been no official comment, but rumor has it that the three top executives were given the option to resign. If they didn't, they'd be fired. My source tells me that Madigan, flanked by his assistants and his attorney, stormed the Exotica offices and delivered the ultimatum himself. What do you think about that?"

"Withdrawing all ads at this stage will cost Exotica a fortune. What do you think they're up to?"

"Trying to avoid a lawsuit, that's what. My guess is they'll remove the litigious claims from the ads and start all over. That'll cost less than losing a lawsuit to us."

Rachel could visualize Blackie storming the Exotica offices. For a moment she almost felt proud of him—until she remembered that he had purchased the notorious company in the first place. It was a little late to try to make amends, if that's what he was doing. More likely he was attempting to prevent litigation.

At home she cuddled with her pets. The warm, silken bodies, the purring, the rough tongues rasping over her hands, acted like a balm to her wounded soul. If she had been smart, she would have reserved her affection for these loyal creatures alone. She would have spared herself the pain that now ripped her insides.

Again she ignored the ringing telephone, and again she went upstairs to lie on her bed and stare into the darkness, mourning that which might have been.

"Rachel, I have to talk to you."

Evan's voice. She had given him a key to her house, which he had obviously used. She sat up and turned on the light. "Come in."

He came in, sat beside her on the bed, and held her hand in his. "Why didn't you answer your phone? You had me worried."

"Because I don't want to talk to Blackie."

"He isn't the only one calling you, sugar."

"I'm sorry."

"What's the trouble between you two?"

"It's complicated."

"Well, I gathered that much from Blackie. The man's hurting bad, sugar. We recorded a blues number today. You should have heard him play. It was enough to snap the strings on a bass fiddle, and you know how strong they are."

"Don't you think I'm hurt too?"

"Of course you are. What I don't understand is why. You two obviously love each other. A blind man could see that. And when two people love each other, nothing's impossible to forgive or overcome."

"You're right about one thing. I love Blackie. But he doesn't love me!"

"Yes, he does."

"Well, he never told me so. Besides, if he loved me, he never would have bought a company that's been trying to destroy everything I've worked for all my adult life. You don't do that to somebody you *like,* much less love." Agitated, Rachel jumped up and paced. "No, you don't do that. That's betrayal."

"Have you heard his side of the story?"

"What can there be to his side of the story that I haven't heard already? Some lame excuse? Spare me."

"It could be the truth."

"The bottom line is that Blackie is on the side of the enemy. For all I know he *is* the enemy, and I'm not charitable enough to love my enemy. I'm sorry, but I'm not."

"If he proves that he's not the enemy, will you talk to the man? Give him a chance?"

"Evan, you're not a businessman. He owns Exotica. There's nothing else to prove," she maintained.

"True, I don't know anything about business, but I know human nature, and I've lived long enough to know that you can't do violence to the human heart and have any kind of peace or happiness. Now, if you want to be miserable the rest of your life, don't give the man you love a chance to fix whatever's wrong."

Evan raised a hand to stop her outburst. "I for one don't believe that Blackie can't fix or explain the problem, and I don't think you're so stubborn or so dumb that you'd give up happiness for the sake of pride or some dry old principle. At least I hope you aren't."

He stood and walked to the door. "There's one other thing. Donna and I are getting married. Saturday night. Just a small ceremony. We want you there, Rachel, but it's only fair to tell you that Blackie will be there too. Will you come?"

"Married?" Rachel echoed in surprise. "I thought you two were just going to live together."

"Well, we decided to go all the way. Can we count on you to help us celebrate, to be Donna's matron of honor? Blackie has agreed to be my best man."

"Yes." Rachel lifted her chin. "If he can stand it, so can I."

"Good. Have you eaten?"

"No. At least I don't think so."

"That's what I thought. I stopped at Armando's and picked up an order of pasta. It's in the kitchen. Come downstairs with me," Evan said.

Her father's concern for her well-being touched her. She walked down the stairs with him. Hugging her warmly before he left, he added, "Think about what I said."

Rachel wandered into the kitchen. As she opened the take-out container, the tempting aroma of tomatoes, herbs, and cheese made her mouth water. She couldn't remember eating anything all day or the day before. Pasta was comfort food, and if there was one thing she needed, it was comfort.

While she ate, she thought about what her father had said. She thought about Blackie. But then, she always thought about him. She couldn't help herself. Could Evan be right in claiming that Blackie loved her? That would be the biggest irony of all, because it wouldn't change anything.

Her doorbell rang. Rachel forced herself to walk slowly to the door. When she saw who it was, she felt a twinge of disappointment.

"Sam, what brings you here after hours?"

"You, not answering your phone."

"I'm sorry."

"I was in the neighborhood anyway, so I thought I'd

stop by with the latest from Exotica, seeing how hard you've been taking all this. Are you personally involved somehow?"

When Rachel didn't answer, Sam continued. "Anyway, I met with Obsidian's lawyer, Ben Madigan. He asked us to wait five working days before bringing suit. He believes they'll come up with a plan that'll spare us the trouble of a court case."

"Do you believe him?"

"That they're trying to come up with a plan? Yes. They may not succeed, but I believe they're serious about finding a way to spare us all a lawsuit."

"It'll be interesting to see their proposal," Rachel forced herself to say.

"Yeah. Are you coming down with something? You look pale and worn out."

"I'm a little under the weather." Lack of sleep and food, not to mention heartbreak and hopelessness, did that to a person. She half heard his remedies for tiredness as she saw him out the door.

Rachel decided to take a long bath, hoping it would relax her. When she was halfway up the stairs, the doorbell rang again. Now what, she wondered tiredly.

The deliveryman handed her a manila envelope, which reminded her of Blackie's "Apology." Her heart beat faster, even though she told herself that no matter what it contained, it wouldn't even begin to solve their problems.

What it did contain was an audiocassette labeled *Blackie's Lament* and a small plastic envelope with tiny green sprigs. The lettering read: *Fresh herbs. Rosemary for remembrance. Blackie.*

Rachel squeezed her eyes tightly against the tears that rose unbidden. She opened the envelope. Then she hurried into the living room to listen to the tape. She sat on the floor without moving until the number ended.

She clasped her arms around her drawn-up knees. Evan had been right. "Blackie's Lament" would soften the heart of the fiercest music hater. Her face was wet with tears. For a woman who had prided herself on rarely crying since she was fifteen, she was rapidly making up for lost time.

Though Rachel knew from experience that a musician's word could not always be believed, his music could. And from his music she knew that Blackie's suffering was as deep as her own. That realization didn't solve their problems, but it brought a small measure of solace to her aching heart and soul. That night she managed to sleep for several hours.

Rachel sat in her car for long minutes, working up her courage to enter the church. All week she had vacillated between anticipation and dread. She missed Blackie so much that she ached for a glimpse of him, but at the same time she knew that that wouldn't be nearly enough. It would be like giving a chocolate lover a tiny sliver of the delicious confection, or letting an opera fan hear only the opening words of a great aria.

The side door of the church opened. The tall figure outlined against the light spilling out behind him was unmistakably the man she loved. Her hungry eyes took in every detail. She couldn't see his features, but he looked thinner in the dark suit he wore. Rachel knew she had lost weight too in the week they had been apart. The second figure joining Blackie was her father.

Realizing that they were worried about her being late, she checked her appearance in the mirror. Thank heaven for makeup, she thought. It almost hid the dark circles under her eyes. It couldn't do anything for the haunted expression in them, unfortunately.

Taking a deep breath, she stepped out of the security of her car. Although it was a relatively short walk to the door where the two men stood, it seemed to take forever. Being conscious of both of them watching her did not make it easier.

"Hi, sugar," Evan greeted her. "Donna was getting worried that she might have to get married without a matron of honor. Come on. She has your flowers."

"Rachel."

Blackie's low, rich voice flowed over her like a sweet melody, soft and caressing. She tightened her hands around the small evening purse she carried to hide their betraying trembling. This was going to be infinitely harder than she had anticipated.

"Hello, Blackie," she managed to say with considerable effort.

As they walked to where Donna was waiting for them, Rachel stole a furtive glance at Blackie. He looked as though he hadn't been sleeping either. The reasons for his insomnia, though, were mostly business related, she suspected. Trying to untangle Exotica's unsavory machinations had to be frustrating and exhausting. Their gazes met—no, collided. His blue eyes pierced her.

Rachel recoiled from the raw pain and longing she saw in his eyes. She clamped her teeth together to stop the words that she knew would be filled with protestations, compassion, and love.

Chapter Twelve

U sing every ounce of discipline and self-control she possessed, Rachel managed to last through the ceremony without breaking down. When Donna and Evan pledged their vows, though, a leaden lump the size of a wrecking ball settled on her chest, causing a dull, steady pain to radiate through her whole body. At least it kept her from bursting into tears. There was a lot to be said for that.

The wedding festivities conspired to keep Blackie by her side. After the ceremony he escorted her to the waiting limousine, her arm linked through his firmly, her dress brushing against his leg. Her body reacted as if it had been programmed for his touch, growing warm and expectant, weak and trembly.

They were seated next to each other at dinner. It was the longest meal Rachel had ever suffered through. Although the lobster was tender enough to be gummed by a toothless crone, Rachel could not swallow more than the first bite. After pushing her food around on her plate for a while, she gave up all pretense of eating. She pasted a smile onto her face, praying she wouldn't mar the happiness of this wedding feast. With her peripheral vision she saw that Blackie wasn't eating either. That almost defeated her. She couldn't stand to see him suffer, no matter what he had or had not done.

After the bride and groom danced the traditional waltz, other couples crowded onto the small dance floor. Fearing that Blackie would ask her to dance, Rachel fled to the foyer of the hotel, staying there until Evan came looking for her.

"Rachel, you can't hide here all evening," Evan chided her gently.

"I know, but I need just a little more time," she pleaded.

"You're going to have to talk to Blackie eventually, so why not get it over with? Can't you see how unhappy he is?"

"Yes. That's what makes it so hard. If he were indifferent or angry or arrogant or anything except hurt, I could pretend indifference myself. I could be coolly polite and speak to him, but as it is, I'm afraid I'll go to pieces and make an absolute fool of myself."

"Hey, sometimes it's okay to do that."

Rachel shook her head. "Nothing's been resolved. Nothing's different."

"Have you given the man a chance to explain? You owe that much even to an enemy. Think how much more you owe to the man you love and who loves you."

Cut to the quick, Rachel met Evan's sympathetic gaze. Her father was right. Blackie deserved a chance to explain. If the roles were reversed, she would like a chance to speak on her own behalf.

"Will you listen to what he has to say?"

Rachel nodded.

"Good. He's waiting for you out by the swimming pool. Come, I'll walk you to the door."

"You had this all set up, didn't you?"

"Sometimes Cupid needs a helping hand." Evan laid an arm around Rachel's shoulders lovingly and led her down the corridor. He held the door open. "Remember that you two love each other. That's more important than anything else," he instructed.

Before Rachel could change her mind, the door clicked shut behind her. Too late. Blackie stood less than six feet away, waiting. They had the dimly lit pool area to themselves.

He unbuttoned his suit jacket. Jamming both hands into his pockets, he faced her. Neither spoke. Finally he said, "You look beautiful. Even more beautiful than I remembered."

Rachel shook her head, indicating she didn't want to hear that.

"I've waited for this chance all week, and now I don't know where to begin," he admitted. He ran a hand through his hair. "Rachel, I've missed you more than I thought it was possible to miss anyone. I simply can't live without you," he said, and he took several steps toward her.

"Please don't touch me," she pleaded, lifting a hand to stop him. "Please don't."

"Why not?"

"Because I'm afraid I'll fall apart, and once I start crying, I don't know if I can stop."

Blackie groaned. "Rachel. You say that to me and expect me to stay away from you? I'm merely flesh and blood, not stone." He uttered a strangled sound and turned away from her, as if to gain control over his emotions. The faint music from the wedding party reached them mutedly.

After a while he turned back to her. "All right. I won't touch you. Let me say a few things first. In a couple of days I'll have a solution to the Exotica mess. I could simply sell the company, but that would only be a temporary measure, and next month or next year they would bother you again, and I won't have that. I want to come up with a permanent solution."

He paced a few steps and then came back to stand in front of her. "Honest to God, I did not know that I owned that lousy company. Ben tried to tell me, but I was so taken with you and the recording that I ignored him."

He paused and shook his head. "My fault. When I started playing with the Gregory Sextet, I let business slide. When I met you, it got away from me entirely. I turned it over to subordinates, and that was inexcusable. I should have given it the care it needed or gotten out of it. I did neither."

Rachel watched him closely as he spoke, and she

believed him not only because she wanted to, but because her visceral reaction told her she was hearing the truth.

"What is even more inexcusable is that by letting things slide, I hurt you badly. Rachel, I would rather die than hurt you. That I swear to you. Do you believe me?"

She inclined her head yes.

"That's more than I deserve," Blackie said, his voice raw. "If it's any comfort to you, I've been more miserable than I knew it was possible to be. I've never felt so unhappy, so absolutely rotten in my whole life."

That she understood, having felt the same way.

"Until I can solve the problems with Exotica, will you wait for me without writing me off? Please, Rachel. I can't make it without you. I wouldn't want to even if I could."

Rachel couldn't speak. She wanted to hurl herself into his arms and kiss him until they both ceased to be.

"Will you keep a good thought for me?"

"Yes," she whispered. "I will."

Visibly moved, Blackie swallowed several times before he could speak. "That's more than I deserve."

Rachel moved forward and touched his arm quickly, briefly, before she tore herself away and ran into the building. She didn't stop inside to say good-bye to Evan and Donna. She couldn't. She was holding on to her composure with the last shreds of her willpower. Running straight to her car, she leaned her forehead against the steering wheel to catch her breath.

She drove slowly, carefully, knowing that her emotions were swaying out of kilter and that it was difficult for her to concentrate. Passing a Walgreen's drugstore, Rachel pulled into the parking lot. She bought a card, wrote a few words of explanation, drove to Evan's apartment, and slipped it under the door. She didn't want the newlyweds to worry about her.

Blackie said he needed a couple of days to straighten things out. Did he mean two? If so, by Monday she might know his solution. Of course, people often said "a couple" when they meant several. However long it took, Blackie seemed to think he could make things right between them. She prayed with all her heart that he could.

Perhaps she was a fool, but she believed his explanation about Exotica. If only she had insisted on answers about his day job, if only . . . Rachel stopped the fruitless second-guessing. Trying to stay away from him because she was so strongly attracted to him had robbed her of the chance to learn about his past. Ironically, avoiding him hadn't worked. She'd fallen in love with him anyway.

She had been home only long enough to exchange her moss green silk dress for a robe when the phone shrilled. It was Blackie.

"Did you get home okay?" he asked.

"Yes, thank you."

"I called so I could tell Evan and Donna not to worry. No, that's not entirely true. I also called because I wanted to make certain you were okay and because I wanted to speak to you again."

"Well, I'm okay." She told him about leaving the card at Evan's place.

"You're beautiful, Rachel. Inside and out. And too good for me. But that isn't going to stop me from trying to make you mine. You hear me?"

"Yes," she said somewhat breathlessly.

"It's easier to talk to you on the phone. I don't have your sweet face to distract me. It kills me to look at you, knowing that you're disappointed and angry with me. It hurts to look at you when I know I caused you pain."

"Are you staying long at the wedding?" she asked, her voice soft.

"No. I'm going in to say good-bye as soon as I hang up. I've scheduled a meeting with my assistants."

"Tonight? Won't they object to working on a Saturday night?"

"Not with the bonuses I'm paying them. I'm in a hurry to remove the obstacle that's standing between us. I assume it's only the Exotica fiasco—that you no longer hold it against me that I'm a musician?"

"Well, you're certainly not impecunious. And you have roots in the city, so you're not footloose. As to—"

"Fickle? I'm not. You're the only woman in my life. The only one I want."

He was making love to her with words, Rachel realized, her cheeks growing warm, her heart beating fast.

"I miss you. Start thinking what you want us to do with the rest of our lives."

Blackie hung up without another word, leaving Rachel hanging on that ambiguous statement. Was he implying they would share their lives? On what basis? Not that it really mattered. What mattered was that they would be together. For the first time in a week, she smiled. Hope rose in her, joyous and triumphant.

The cautious streak in her nature, though, caused her to rein in her wild joy and contain it with prudent reservations. Everything was still hypothetical. Nothing had been settled definitely.

She felt the need for action, for movement. After re-dressing in running shoes and a sweat suit, she took Piccolo for a run through the quiet neighborhood.

On Monday morning Rachel was tempted to go to the office early, but knowing that there wouldn't be any news, she forced herself to take care of a few chores around the house.

At nine-thirty Sam telephoned, telling her that Blackstone Madigan had called a press conference for eleven. A short segment of it would be featured on the twelve-thirty edition of *Business Around Town,* a local television program. Rachel eagerly agreed to attend the press conference. She knew she couldn't wait for the televised version.

At the office she was too nervous to tackle any big projects, so she tidied her desk, dictated letters, and looked at proposals for the new animal shelter. That cashier's check for ten thousand dollars enabled them to go ahead with buying the first of three new shelters.

Suddenly Rachel sat very still. She knew who had donated the money. Leaning back in her chair, she thought back to that day.

Blackie had been there almost the whole time and had had ample opportunities to slip it into the cash box. It couldn't have been anyone else. Was it any wonder that she loved him so?

Great tenderness for him filled her heart and soul. Rachel spent the rest of the morning daydreaming about Blackie until Sam came for her.

Even though she wore high-heeled shoes, Rachel insisted that they walk to Obsidian's headquarters. It was silly to take a cab only a few blocks. Besides, she felt so restless with anticipation that she needed the exercise.

The small conference room was already crowded. A security guard led them to seats in the back of the room, which suited Rachel perfectly. When Blackie took the speaker's stand, the talking ceased. Handsome in a light gray suit, he scanned the crowd. His search stopped when he found Rachel. It seemed to her that when he spoke, he spoke to her alone.

His announcements were simple, and, as with most simple things, they were forceful in their clarity and brevity. Obsidian International had been reorganized. It would be governed by a board of regents with Blackie presiding over their monthly meetings. The day-to-day operations would be carried out by two directors— Curtis Shafer and George Baldwin.

As for Exotica Cosmetics, the new policy redirected the company's efforts to the production of the original products for which it was famous until a new management team could be appointed. As of that morning, Blackie announced, Exotica had ceased the production of all imitation perfumes.

Rachel was stunned. The excited murmuring that filled the room indicated that she was not the only one so affected. To Sam she said, "He can't do that. The company will lose millions."

Sam patted her arm reassuringly. "He knows what he's doing. Don't worry about him."

Maybe so, Rachel thought worriedly, but their various imitation perfumes had to have constituted a good chunk of Exotica's sales. She couldn't bear the idea of Blackie's risking everything he had worked for.

Blackie opened the floor to questions. He freely admitted relinquishing control of Obsidian International because he wanted to concentrate on music, particularly the writing and producing of jazz.

Rachel had to talk to him. There were a million things she wanted to ask him, to tell him. She also wanted to hug and kiss him and . . .

Quickly she stopped her thoughts from straying too far. On a sheet of paper she wrote, *I have to see you. We have to see you.* Under the message she drew the stick figure of a woman, three circles with whiskers, and one with a wagging tail. She folded the note and asked the security guard to deliver it to Blackie. She waited almost breathlessly for him to read it.

When he did, a delighted smile curved his lips. He looked straight at Rachel when he spoke. "The answer to this particular question is, yes, Exotica will meet with Athena at five to discuss past differences. I relish the idea of resolving our difficulties."

Rachel smiled back at Blackie, heedless of Sam's curious look. "Let's go," she said.

Outside Sam asked, "What was all that about? If you're meeting with Exotica, I, as your attorney, should be present."

"Not a chance, Sam." She grinned at his perplexed expression. "This is personal. Blackstone and I have a few things to settle, woman to man."

"I knew it," Sam said. "I knew there was more to it than just business."

"A whole lot more." Rachel smiled enigmatically, refusing to say another word on the subject.

Rachel left her office at three. She couldn't sit still another moment. Not that she had accomplished anything anyway. Not when she kept hearing Blackie's sonorous voice telling her that he relished the idea of resolving their difficulties.

She would spend the two intervening hours preparing a feast. There wasn't time to bake bread from scratch, but she had some loaves in the freezer that always turned out deliciously. Cleaning vegetables for a curry, steaming the kasha, and preparing raspberries for dessert kept her body busy and her thoughts and anticipation in check.

When the doorbell rang, she ran to open the door,

thinking it must a deliveryman or possibly the postman. It wasn't.

"It's not five," she said when she found her voice.

"I know. I couldn't wait any longer." Blackie came inside and closed the door behind him.

"I was going to go upstairs and get cleaned up and put on a nice dress and—"

"Why? You look lovely in everything you wear."

"Oh." Rachel watched him toss his jacket and his tie over the umbrella stand. A tingling sensation started at the base of her spine and worked its way upward.

"During the past week I've discovered a number of things, the most important of which is that I love you," he said, standing in front of her. "I've felt that way about you for quite a while, but I was afraid to put a name to the feeling, thinking that by labeling it I would lessen it. I haven't. Nothing can lessen it."

"I know," Rachel said.

"Everybody knew that I loved you except me. Sometimes I can be very dense."

"You knew. Deep down you knew."

"Yes." It was true, he realized, amazed.

Rachel raised her face for his kiss. It rocked them with the force of an explosion.

"It's been so long," Blackie murmured against her mouth. "So long."

"Yes," she said simply. Their melody, slightly different but even more potent than before, flowed over them, drowning out everything else.

They emerged breathless but smiling from the long kiss.

The first thing Blackie said rendered Rachel speechless.

"Will you marry me?" he repeated.

"Are you sure you want to get married?"

"I thought I heard the music of the spheres and hallelujah choruses while we kissed, so, yes, I'm sure." He grinned at her.

"I thought you favored living together."

"Nope. I'm talking marriage." Gently he moved the strand of dark hair that had fallen over her cheek.

"Marriage."

"Yup. You know, that which comes after a ceremony like the one we witnessed Saturday night?"

"But why? The one time we talked of marriage, you said you came to your senses just in time to prevent such a disaster."

"That's because she wasn't the right woman. You are." He looked at her searchingly. "I know on the surface I might not seem like suitable husband material, but if you look more closely, you'll find that I meet all the qualifications you mentioned. I love you. I want to care for you. I want to share my life with you and only you. Of course, that includes the assorted creatures in your life. But there will be no other woman ever except you. And I want it all sanctified before God and man."

Rachel felt so overwhelmed, she couldn't speak.

"Did I leave out any qualifications?"

She shook her head.

"How do I stack up as husband material?" he asked.

He was serious. Blackie meant every word he had said, she realized with wonder. Her insides rocked with joy. She wanted to shout, to laugh, to cry.

She bit her lip to gain a semblance of self-control. "You're the most perfect husband material I've ever come across." Then her joy erupted and poured over him. "I love you, and, yes, I'll marry you."

They hugged and laughed and danced through the kitchen like happy children.

When they calmed down a little, Rachel's expression became serious. "Blackie, have you looked at Exotica's finances carefully? Can you discontinue the imitation fragrances without going bankrupt? I know I said some harsh things about that company, but I don't want to see it go under. All those people without jobs—"

Blackie laid a silencing finger across her lips.

"First, the profits from the imitations were much less than expected. Second, by focusing on the stock items that have sold steadily over the years, a smart director could come up with a good ad campaign and double their sales. Third, by discontinuing all covert operations and concentrating on developing new products, profits will exceed those made on the counterfeit scents."

Rachel looked at him, her eyes shining with admiration. "You did investigate everything. All you need now is a good director."

"No problem. I've got a name already. All she has to do is agree."

"Who?"

"You."

"Me?"

"I'm giving you my controlling shares of Exotica as a wedding present. You're perfect for the job. If you're worried about divided loyalties, don't be. I've talked with Laura. She said she would be interested in a merger as long as you took charge of Exotica."

For long seconds all Rachel could do was stare at Blackie. "In my wildest dreams that's the one thing I never expected."

"It's the best possible solution. Think about it."

Rachel did. "But—"

He cut her off with a kiss. "You yourself pointed out that I know little about the cosmetics industry. If I have to manage Exotica, I'll be in the same spot as before, holding down two jobs, trying to be the best husband possible, and not having the time I need for—"

"That does it. You're not working two jobs, and that's final. If it means your being an overworked and absent husband, I'll take care of Exotica," Rachel declared staunchly.

"I hoped you'd say that." Blackie pulled her closer against him, stroking the silken hair he loved. "Where do you want to live? Here? In the loft? In a condominium overlooking the lake? In a house in the suburbs?"

"Here in my house, if you don't mind. Old One-Eye—that is, Cy—will like it here too. After the house is fixed up, it'll be really nice," Rachel assured him.

"That's fine with me. I like it here. As a matter of fact, you'll find that I'm right handy around the house."

"I knew you would be," Rachel said with a grin. Tucked in the sheltering arms of the man she loved, she closed her eyes in complete bliss. She listened to the melody Blackie hummed.

" 'Heartsong.' That's what I'll call it," he murmured.

"That's perfect," Rachel agreed. *Heartsong.* The name of their own, private melody of love.